TALES OF RESISTANCE

Tales

of

Resistance

–Peter Leach–

Winner of the 1998
George Garrett Fiction Prize

Texas Review Press
Huntsville, Texs

FIRST EDITION, 1999

Requests for permission to reproduce material from this work should be sent to:

Permissions
Texas Review Press
English Department
Sam Houston State University
Huntsville, TX 77341-2146

Acknowledgments

My thanks to the following publications where stories first appeared:

River Styx for "The Man I Threw Out the Window," *Nebraska Review* for "The Convict's Tale," *Louisville Review* for "Eight Ball," *Minnesota Review* for "Strawberries," *Aloe* for "Deer in June," *Artful Dodge* for "Of Human Sacrifice," and *Virginia Quarterly Review* for "The Fish Trap," later reprinted in *Prize Stories 1974: The O. Henry Awards.*

Cover design and art by Kit Keith

Library of Congress Cataloging-in-Publication Data

Leach, Peter, 1935-
    Tales of resistance / Peter Leach.
        p.   cm.
    ISBN 1-881515-21-4 (pbk.)
    1. United States--Social life and customs--20th century--Fiction.
I. Title.
PS3562.E176T35   1999
813'.54--dc21   99-27190
                                                 CIP

TABLE OF CONTENTS

THE BALL PLAYERS — 1

THE CONVICT'S TALE — 13

CROPPERS ON THE HIGHWAY — 23

DEER IN JUNE — 30

EIGHT BALL — 37

THE FISH TRAP — 48

OF HUMAN SACRIFICE — 55

A JUDGE'S TALE — 66

STRAWBERRIES — 75

THE MAN I THREW OUT THE WINDOW — 86

FOR MY FATHER,
JACK LEACH

The Ball Players

I come to Festus because a fellow I went to grade school with we played a lot of ball together and he become superintendent at Sealed Beam. I decided I wasn't going to play professional baseball any more and had got a bread route in south St. Louis where a lot of people knew me and I was interested in that kind of work and making pretty good money, although I was playing Sunday ball for the railroad shops.

So Ben Politte was a superintendent and over the baseball team for Sealed Beam at Festus and he come up to St. Louis and asked me if I would take a job. I told him I was pretty well satisfied with my bread route. "Well," he said, "will you come down and interview? We'll make it worth your while."

I decided I would talk to them since Ben was a friend of mine and I went down and they told me what they would give me and I wasn't satisfied with it. They brought in the employment manager and then the general manager, and finally we go in to see Mr. Desloge that they said was a star shortstop at Princeton College and for a time played semi-pro ball himself.

He shook my hand and said he heard of me how I played triple-A ball at Spartanburg and hit twenty-six home runs and they called me the Babe Ruth of the Bushes and was in the Texas League and hit against Dizzy Dean. I did too hit a home run off Dizzy Dean at Shreveport, Louisiana, of course before he come up to St. Louis and become the great Dizzy Dean. He was just a kid then like me and I was nineteen years old.

Mr. Desloge took me to the window of his office there that looked down on the company ball field on the bottom land up against the bluff. It was just the nicest little stadium grandstand tucked up into the hollow and concrete bleachers in the shade of the cotton-wood trees bluegrass field and the dirt mound and base paths. I played in parks in triple-A that was cow pastures by comparison. He sweet-talked me saying how he played a little ball himself before he took a fall off a horse. Crippled his hip they said from a horse rolled over on him playing polo at the St. Louis Country Club and he worked to develop his upper body strength. Carried a revolver in a kidskin shoulder holster—I seen it—and he took a personal interest in the ball players, and he shook my hand and says they would make it worth my time.

I decided I would go to work for him.

I was hired as a buffer and polisher which was one of the highest paid classifications outside the tool and die makers at Sealed Beam. I found out later I was being paid some over and above my classification and me and the other ballplayers they was giving us special treatment. We could clock in late the morning after an industrial league game that we won and not get fired, take batting practice an afternoon before a game while we was still clocked in. Now and then Mr. Desloge might give us five dollars for a steak dinner and a picture show. He would walk down the line with his cane, stop and slap the ballplayers on the back, pat you on the butt.

We ball players was preferred employees, the fair-haired boys.

So I can see how the people involved in the sit-down was reluctant to talk to me for the reason I was a ball player. The first I knew about it was Rex Roberts he says to me, "Stan, at nine o'clock a.m. we are going to shut this place down."

I say, "I'm with you."   •

"Is that so?" says Rex.

I tell him some of the ball players was talking about it and we seen how other people was treated and we decided whatever come down we was going to participate—Jack Jourdan, Jim Tobin, Von Burgen, Dale Pugh, Owen Pugh and two other guys. That's not all of the ball players. The rest they was on the management side, pretty boys for Mr. Desloge.

"I give you fair warning, Stan."

By now Big Riley Etchison is listening and some of the other fellows stand around waiting for the line to start up.

"I'm trying to tell you, Rex," I say, "Count me in on it."

Big Riley says, "Show me a ball player, and I will show you a rat." I could ask him You calling me a rat? but I let it pass.

A fellow named Will Murdoch says, "Mr. Desloge is always looking for the boys who can play ball."

"Play ball with management," another fellow says.

"Look," I say, "let me tell you about the candy room."

"Candy room, candy ass," Riley says and I don't care how big he is, I am looking at my wheel wrench on the die cart beside him and he is that close to getting his head knocked off.

"Ball players don't go to the candy room," says Murdoch.

"Let me tell you," I say. "I come in one day last week and this lard ass I ain't never seen before says the regular man is out sick and today he is the boss of our line. That's Rendleman. He says to us, 'Well, you go to the candy room and if we get some lamps in I'll come and get you.'"

"Tell us about it, Stan," Big Riley says.

I did.

The candy room was just a little room up in front where a guy sold candy and chewing gum and milk and things. You have to ring your clock card out and sit down there maybe until noon or after. You could sit from 7:30 or eight o'clock until one o'clock in the candy room. My friend Rose Byers and some of them from a line that was mostly women and a jackass foreman named Hobeson . . . there has been times when they set in there for all day and never get a job of work to do, and she told me maybe it was four or five dollars on her check for two whole weeks. Fellows say if you go home even step out for a smoke or take a leak and your foreman comes looking and don't find you, you're fired.

I tell them, "So Rendleman says, 'Well, we'll be ready to start up at one o'clock.'"

"What day was that?" Rex asks.

"Thursday . . . . We set in there five hours."

"Welcome to the club, Stan."

"Rendleman didn't know you was a ball player."

"I'm not going to tell him."

"Why not?"

It is one thing for them to show you favoritism and you can't help it but what if I was to pipe up and say oh I am a ball player and you can't do me like that? I just shake my head.

Big Riley and Murdoch look at each other like they are making up their minds.

"Then I got fired."

I tell them about it.

After we finally was at work again to get paid for it I go in the wash room and have a smoke which I know is against the rules and regulations even for ball players. I come back and Rendleman says to me, "You were six and a half minutes."

I say, "Was I?"

"Five is enough."

I ask him, "What are you going to do about it?"

"You're fired."

"I'm fired?" I say.

"There's the door and a man waiting for your job."

I went and got my coat and was leaving when my friend **Ben Politte** that was the boss of this individual says, "Where you going?"

I say, "I was fired."

He says, "Who fired you?" I told him and he says, "He can't fire you. Go on back to work."

So I went back to the line and put my apron on and started in at my buffing lathe that I just left.

"Old Ben saved your ass," Murdoch says.

"I shouldn't ought to need Ben to save my ass," I say. "Time you in the can . . . ! It ain't right."

Rex looks around as if he is waiting for anyone to object and then he says to me, "All right, Stan, I'll see if we can find something for you to do."

So the time come and Rex told me my first assignment and that was to see that all the buffing in my area after the lathes and everything was shut down. We would take the reflector cones off the conveyor belt after they was in the chrome bath and buff them on the buffing wheels on the lathes and put them back on the conveyor. Well that lard ass Rendleman that had stayed on as the regular foreman for our line he just hauled on out of there and I didn't have no problem. The majority of the buffers in our group was sympathetic to the cause and our lathes was among the first to shut down.

My next assignment was from Big Riley Etchison that was a buffer too but over in another group and he says, "I've got a job for you, Stan. Only I want you to be careful and not get hurt."

I didn't want him to think I was scared so I said, "What is it?"

"You see that switch up there on the wall?" he says.

I said, "I see it."

He says, "I want you to pick up your wheel wrench and go over and pull the switch and then stand there by that switch and if anybody tries to turn it back on, knock their damn head off."

Well a wheel wrench is a big iron bar about so long with a curve on the end that you use to tighten and loosen the nuts on your buffing wheels on your lathe.

"Riley," I says, "you don't want me doing this."

What I am scared of is I will hurt somebody and go to prison, or a friend of mine will come and try to turn that switch on.

"You're a contrary fellow, Stan," he says.

I think he is all friendly now like calling me a candy ass is water over the dam.

"You was ready to take that wheel wrench to me, wasn't you?"

"Called me a candy ass."

"That's the spirit, Stan . . . . Management thinks we're all candy ass."

I get the heft of my wheel wrench and walk over to the big switch and pull it.

I have cast my lot.

You can just hear that plant getting quieter and quieter because the machines was going down.

Now there was this friend of mine, Rose Byers, ninety pounds wringing wet and she had a nervous breakdown when she finished in the Normal School and went to work at Sealed Beam as an inspector up on the balcony in one of the lines that was still working. She come to all the ball games and cheered like crazy and brung her two sisters and all their girlfriends. We called her Mary Contrary because she was always jumping the umpire and the other team calling them names—you are surprised at a little lady like that. She told me she never had a clue.

Her job was to run a machine that put grommets on the end of wires. She was sitting there running the machine when a fellow that was quite a cut-up, Jay Vance, he come and shut her machine off and she thought he was cutting up. She reached over and turned it back on and he turned it off again. She turned it back on the third time and he said, "Mary, don't turn your machine on any more. This is a strike."

She says, "What are you talking about? A strike? What's that?"

He told her, "This here is a sit-down strike. The men that are with us are going to stay in here and close everything down but all the women will have to walk out."

This was going off pretty good in our buffing department but back on some of the lines we had a lot of women working where they was assembling headlights and it was a little more hectic. A great big guy by the name of Hobeson thought he was pretty hot stuff keeps his line running. When somebody turns his belt off he just goes and turns it back on. "You go back to work," he tells the girls. "There ain't going to be no strike here."

Somebody says, "We're going to have to get that fellow out of there." So Big Will Murdoch from our group and Big Riley Etchison and me and Rex we went on back to the assembly lines where the belts was still running and told this fellow Hobeson to close down. Big Riley says, "Shut her down."

And Hobeson says to Riley, "Look, this is my line. I'll take care of it."

Riley he goes up to Hobeson and he says, "Now I'm going to turn that off. Don't you even attempt to turn it back on or we'll knock your head off." Riley reaches over and jerks the lever that shuts down the line and says, "You better get going."

Of course there was several more of our guys around.

Hobeson didn't turn it on no more, decided it would be best for his health I think to leave. He left. He made himself scarce and it wasn't long until there wasn't a machine running in Sealed Beam. We told the women they all had to leave. They was married women, single women and married men, single men. We didn't want to get into anything that might not look good, so by four o'clock all the women was out of there. Let's face it, you couldn't have men and women staying in the plant together overnight.

Mary and them went across Sulphur Street to Mom and Pop's Cafe and begun preparing sandwiches and hot meals for us.

Mary was living at home and her father was in supervision, a foreman at Safety Glass and anti-union like the Mayor and police and near the whole town—out of 2000 at Sealed Beam only 200 of us was sit-downers. The rest the Company called them the Loyal 2000, give them chrome-plated badges that says LOYAL 2000.

So Mary's dad when he hears she is cooking hot meals for the boys and taking it in to them, he asks her and she says she's not going to lie to him. He says to her, "As long as you are living under my roof, there will be no aid and comfort to them sonsofbitches on your part."

Her mom is crying, ironing her dad's shirt.

Mary went and stayed with her sister that was a chambermaid at the Railroad Hotel.

Now during this time people was making up their minds and like I said when all was said and done there was the Loyal 2000 and the rest of us the 200 hard heads that was determined to sit down and keep the plant shut. As the machines shut off and there was a silence, a number of them noticed me and the Pugh brothers and Jim Jourdan and they was surprised and remarked the ball players is in on it. We was favored employees, the fair-haired boys you know, and the guys never trusted us altogether. People remarked on it, "The ball players!" The ideal seemed to be if even the ball players was in on this there must be something to it.

The last of the Loyal 2000 was going on out the door, only they wasn't all Company men by any means. They just decided they was not in for the sit-down and I don't blame them for that. We put ourselves in harm's way. A man that chose not to do that, it is his business. What I can't abide is a rat or a man that holds office in our organization and goes over to the Company side.

We had shut the plant down and not one machine was running and the last of the men that chose not to participate was heading out the gate. I was sitting down with my wheel wrench by the switch that I had shut off drinking coffee out of the cup from my thermos bottle and enjoying myself.

Then my buddy from way back, Ben Politte, that got me on at Sealed Beam, he come by and seen me there and he says, "What the hell are you doing?"

I say, "Drinking my coffee."

He says, "They are running us all out of here. Come on."

I say, "Ben, we're just running you guys out. I'm going to stay."

He says, "Stan, you don't mean that."

I say, "Yes, I mean it."

"We go way back."

"Don't make me cry."

"I got you on here."

"I had me a nice bread route."

"Mr. Desloge treats you right, Stan. You and the ball players."

"That's not just."

Ben shakes his head. "These fellows . . . some of them are all right. But they are misguided. The Reds got to them."

"I don't know about no Reds," I say.

"You're a ball player."

"I just know about the candy room."

"How can you do this to me?"

"And that lard ass Rendleman firing me for six and a half minutes in the can."

"Did I let that go?"

I had run out of smart answers.

"I backed you up. I reamed his ass."

"That was favoritism to me as a star ball player."

"Stan, there's five men at the gate for every job inside here. Somebody offers you a little favoritism, you take it or go hungry."

I shake my head.

"Think about your mother."

I never told Ben about the first job I took after I left Pemiscot County—I was a scab for the Joplin Traction Company. When Mama found out she slapped my face, the only time she ever done that.

"You're all she's got."

"You better haul on out, Ben," I say. "I don't want to see you get hurt."

I had stood up by then and I must have had that wheel wrench up on my shoulder and Ben give me a look I still remember, like I was the most pathetic ungrateful sonofabitch he ever known. He left.

I never would have used the wheel wrench on old Ben. Not even if he tried to turn that switch back on.

IT WAS LIKE a siege in olden days and we got the castle. Other guys that was in sympathy with us outside and the women walked the picket line. The women brought us food right up to the gate and we went down and got it. Management never tried to stop that with only five or six security. The National Guard didn't come in until afterwards. We was in there and if we wanted to we could do a lot of damage.

So the women brought us hot meals—pots of soup and beans and sandwiches. We had the carts that the machinists use when they are taking a broken die back to the shop and we would take these carts —you seen them, the four-wheel carts with a shelf in them and little wheels on casters—and roll them out to the gate and load up what the women had brought in. They'd have beans and other kinds of soup in washtubs for us, big old galvanized iron laundry tubs like for a church social or the Elks Club. We had tin plates and we converted one of the washrooms into a place where we washed dishes. I was on the dish-washing crew at one time. Mary and her friends would sneak along the railroad track and bring us smokes, candy, snuff, things she could reach up to us in the windows that was right along the tracks there.

We all had certain things to do, go to different gates and circulate around, check the windows, things like that. We took turns on the clean-up, keep where we was living neat and tidy. We wasn't destroying nothing in there or leaving a mess.

We made a few little things to protect ourselves, blackjacks out of spring steel and bolts and friction tape. It was a kind of leaf spring they used in the headlamps five or six inches long and we took machine bolts and we had all the friction tape we needed and fastened them together. That's how we made the blackjacks.

The time passed. Some of the guys they'd play euchre. One fellow he could just make an accordian talk and another played the banjo and the women brought their instruments to them and we made music. We sung Joe Hill songs.

We slept back in the shipping department where there was hundreds of big boxes, a lot of them filled with headlamps. The wives had brought over blankets and pillows and we made our bunks on these shipping boxes. Some guys near you was always up and going on patrol so you didn't really sleep that good.

Of course we kept constant patrol. We had regular patrols all down the dock which was right by a railroad track. We got word the police was coming to throw us out of the plant and we had fire hoses in there and we designated people to man different hoses.

You had to get outside once in a while. We'd send people some place to check and see what was going on in town, because we knew Management was stirring up trouble on the outside, furnishing alcohol to the LOYAL 2000 and doing things to get them provoked so they would come in and throw us all out. We knew they had the manpower if the Company could get them to do it but we just said, "Look. Send them in."

I went out several times. I crawled out on the railroad tracks back there and I'd go and circle around the town just to see what the hell was going on and come back in the plant.

One night I go in the Gold Band tavern that was owned by an individual named Schlafly where you could run a tab and cash a check you know and we thought he was a friend of the working man. I have to be careful where I show my face because with a ten-day beard and not smelling too good you can tell pretty quick I must be one of the sit-down guys, and there was a warrant out on us for criminal tresspassing.

Chuck Klein and Oral Hildebrand was in there two of the ball players that chose not to join us and Oral says, "Watch yourself, Stan."

I say, "How's that?"

He says, "I wouldn't trust Schlafly too far."

I look up in the mirror. Schlafly has his eye on me from the other end of the bar.

Oral buys me a Seagrams and a Stag beer. Let me tell you that was nice going down. Then Chuck buys and after that a friend of mine that's not a ball player.

Oral he leans over close to my ear and says, "You fellows need to watch it."

I nod. I am really feeling good for a change.

"They are coming in after you with ax handles."

I just nod. We heard rumors like this.

Chuck Klein tries to catch his eye.

"I'm telling him," Oral says.

That gets my attention. Oral and Chuck that we played ball together for three seasons know something and they wasn't going to tell me.

"When?" I say.

"Any day now," Oral says. "They will sneak up through the old mine tunnels."

WE WAS READY for them. Only it never happened.

If they had got inside on us there would have been a lot of men killed and badly injured because we wasn't going to give up that plant without a battle.

We was very militant. We was ready to go for any damn thing.

When they come to some kind of agreement and the sit-down was ended, I was like a little banty rooster.

We paraded out of that plant onto Dunklin Avenue and right on up to the Armory. If I can recall they had reached some kind of tentative agreement probably in Detroit or Flint and all the sit-downers would evacuate all the plants. Word got down here to us on this particular day we were supposed to relinquish our hold on the plant. And we did. We marched from Sealed Beam up town to the Armory and we held a big mass meeting and rally up there and had a big time.

Our friends and the women were all lined up across Sulphur Street cheering us. We had flags and our rag-tag band and Big Riley with a wheel wrench over his shoulder he led the group out of the plant. Everybody was cheering us. We all had beards . . . and wives were running up to their husbands and the little children running up to their daddies and we all come out making the victory sign.

And a personal note here most of us that were ball players the women smuggled in our uniforms and some bats so the most of us— Jack Jourdan, Jim Tobin, Von Burgen, Dale Pugh, Owen Pugh and two other guys—we had on our industrial league ball uniforms that says SEALED BEAM on them and our names and numbers. My number was 11. We had on our uniform shirts and caps and most of us big old hard-ball bats on our shoulders and people—of course everybody knew by now several of us was in on the sit-down but now they saw for theirselves—and as we marched by they remarked on it, "The ball players!"

I admit I felt proud.

I still do.

BUT TO TELL you the truth so far as Mr. Desloge was concerned— oh, our picture was in the newspaper, the St. Louis newspaper that his friends at the country club all seen—it just added insult to injury.

When we had won recognition and was back on the job, they assigned me with some of the Loyal 2000. Ben Politte calls me over to the side and he says, "Stan, I want you to watch your step. These guys kind of resent what you fellows did."

I ask him, "What the hell do you mean?"

"They don't like losing all that time. Just . . . kind of watch your step."

"Let me tell you something, Ben . . . I don't like how these guys never had the balls to join us and now they reap the benefit. And if any of them gives me a problem, I'll part his damn hair with a wheel wrench."

They know better than to cross my path.

A few days after that the tune has changed. Ben come to me and says, "Hey, Mr. Desloge want to talk to you."

I say, "Talk to me about what?"

He says, "There's a job open."

"Hell, I've got a job."

He acts like he don't understand.

"Well, I'm satisfied."

"I'm glad you're satisfied, but—"

"Are you satisfied with your job?" I ask him.

"Yes," he says.

"You're satisfied. I'm satisfied," I say.

"Well, would you consider taking a job in supervision?" he says.

I say, "Hell, no. You know that, Ben."

"Why not?"

"Let me tell you one reason why," I say. "I can go down through this plant here and those people will say, 'Hi, Stan. How you doing? Hi!' But if you go down there they say, 'Look at that fat old sonofabitch.'"

Me and Ben use to be friends that when you call me that smile you know. Now I'm not so sure.

"See the difference?"

"Mr. Desloge takes an interest," he says.

"Is that so?"

"Calls you his Babe Ruth of the bushes."

"I'm telling you, Ben . . . "

"You can name your price."

"Well I heard from the fellows you let Mr. Desloge take an interest in you, go for a night on the town in St. Louis, you get his Princeton dick up your ass."

"Well, he wants to talk to you," Ben says.

"Even if I'm not interested?"

"He wants to talk to you."

So we go in and see Mr. Desloge again and he is courteous the perfect gentleman and like a good fellow on another team that you just whipped in a game and he says, "Stan Parker . . . my Babe Ruth of the bushes."

"Yes, sir," I say. I am feeling pretty awkward but I am not going to kiss his ass.

"You surprise me, Stan," he says. "I thought you were just another pretty face."

I know when I am being made light of and I keep my smart answer to myself. He was wearing that revolver in the kidskin shoulder holster too, a .32 or a .38.

He says, "You beat us . . . well, I won't say fair and square . . . but you did. You showed firm resolve."

"Thank you, sir," I say.

"That's a quality I value in management."

"My friends value it too," I say.

"I take it Ben told you my offer . . . foreman over the balcony line . . . your friend Rose what's-her-name. It's mostly women."

"We didn't get that specific."

"What would you need to do that?"

"Mr. Desloge, I appreciate your offer," I say. "But I don't see myself in supervision."

"It's the same principle as playing ball, Stan," he says. "You get your people working together as a team."

"Well, sir, that's one way to see it," I say. "But my friends would see it as me going over from our team to yours."

"Friends can hold you back, Stan."

"Or stand by you," I say.

Mr. Desloge looks at me, kind of smiles. "Seventy-five cents," he says. "It would come to better than a hundred and fifty a month."

"That's good money," I say. It was. With incentives I was taking home on the average maybe twenty-five dollars a week. "But what you give me now is what the work is worth."

He looks at me kind of mean like to say well don't count on it. But what he says is, "I respect that."

I reach out, and we shake hands.

"I can't do a thing with him, Mr. Desloge," Ben says. "He is a hard-headed hillbilly from down home."

"We need more of his kind in supervision," Mr. Desloge says with another kind of mean look, this time at Ben.

The next thing they done was to discontinue the ball team and let Ben Politte go since being over the company team is half his job, and I go back to my bread route. Mr. Desloge says we was in on the sit-down and after all he done for us the ball players is just a bunch of ingrates.

The Convict's Tale

This was told to me by M.D. Stokes at the Missouri State Penitentiary in Jefferson City. "You know the story of why so many mens in the jails?" he asked.

I shook my head. We were in the classroom off the basement corridor to McClung or B and C Halls. Stokes is an elderly dining car porter serving a long sentence for Murder Two in a north St. Louis love-triangle situation. He reads extensively in W.E.B. Dubois, Houck's *Spanish Regime*, *The Conspiracy of the Elders of Zion* and other arcane works, and he broods upon them in the night.

"Well, my great-grandfather he work for the railroad laying track," he said. "One he built on name the Old Mines branch up the Forch a Reno. It was abandon they say cause the money run out at Venner Bluff. But the coon-ass hillbillies at the Old Mines didn't study no railroad in there, and they had as a guest Mr. Jesse James.

"The Forch a Reno a bitch of a job, drilling, blasting. Right of way has to wind around all them limestone clifts with cedar trees and little twisted-up oak trees growing on the ledges and in the cracks. Clifts rise up two hundred feet from the green water of the river and most places close enough to throw rocks across. Time they come to Venner Bluff the Captains done already spent twice as much money as they suppose to—even if it was poor folks' taxes for the railroad bonds—and they ready to try most anything.

"Now the way I was told it, the working mens one Sunday afternoon taking they only time off. They laying around drinking some moonshine, smoking the hemp, having a cock fight. They was black and some Chinamens that come to work on the railroads and some Italians and Polish and Irish and Swedes and Germans and Russians. Immigrants fresh off the boat that white Americans treat just about like niggers then anyhow. Be wage slaves. They having some of that distillate of corn and wine from the finest local grapes and blackberries and smoking locally grown cannibis that they obtain from the coon-ass hillbillies of the neighborhood. They betting on the cock-fights in front of the shanty cars and old white pyramid army tents and shacks they be living in on the shelf of land under the bluffs by the new tracks and the river there. Some of them bad mix-race hillbillies down fraternizing among them selling moonshine, selling grass and ass, pimping they women, stealing things, spying on the railroad. Stealing dynamite. And people playing music—mouth organ, banjo, juice harp. Women there too, women and childrens that follow the workingmens. And tomorrow some of the strong womens be laying track. Now they hanging out taking a little pleasure on a Sunday afternoon, when they hear a train whistle way down the valley.

"After a while this three-car work train come in kind of real slow like a strange dog his tail between his legs. Just a engine, a coal car, and one flat car, and some big old crates chain down.

"The Captain come out and say, 'You boys give me a hand on these here crates.'

"Not exactly PDQ, they come and unload the crates.

"All that night the Captain and a man with him name Owens and Owens' boy Kempf they fooling with what was in the crates by lantern light, cursing, hammering, fooling around.

"In the morning, Monday morning, mens and some of the womens come to work at first daylight, they see this contraption there on the tracks. It was on a handcar with hoses and a boiler. Look like a great big iron grasshopper setting there on this handcar. And Owens the professor in a vest with a watch chain and the pimple-face boy Kempf in his cap, they standing there looking at it. The mens coming to work they gather around, nudge each other, whisper, 'What that thing? What's that?'

"Well, what it was was a drill.

"Captain blowing the whistle time to go to work, and nobody thinking much about it.

"You may have heard something like this story. But how you heard it before, you heard it wrong.

"The steam drill just didn't want to work right. Professor Owens and that dirty white boy be messing over it all day. It drill in a few inches, and break down. They mess over it, then drill in a while more. It was just a big old forge hammer hung sideways like a pendulum and this worm gear to raise and let it fall on the drill. Has to have a man hold the drill rod to the hole and turn it every time. The engine don't turn the drill. It just raise the hammer and let it fall, like a pile-driver laid sideways. Give me you pencil . . . . My daddy he draw it for us childrens like that . . . .

"It make about the same noise as a man swinging a sledge

hammer when it hit the drill. Only besides that the steam engine going, 'Whoosh-puht . . . whoosh-puht . . . whoosh—puht . . . .' Sound silly, don't it? That how my daddy say it telling us childrens, 'Whoosh-puht . . . whoosh-puht . . . .'

"Well, Captain he go and ask my great-grandaddy Fort John Stokes to work alongside this drill a while, 'just for comparison.'

"My great-grandaddy he big and strong and half smart. Captains always holding him up as a example. 'Well, Big John he can do it . . . Well, Big John ain't complaining.' You know the type of individual I mean. Yas, SUH!

"So John he commence to drill just like it was a regular day at work. Other mens and womens Captain don't allow just to stand around watching. But all day while they working they hear the steam drill, 'Whoosh-puht . . . BLAM! . . . whoosh-puht . . . BLAM!'

"The coon-ass hillbillies they hear it too and by late in the afternoon, they be watching. Be up on the bluffs and some right down on the tracks watching that drill and Big John. Coon-asses live in the hollows up at View Mean Creek, Terre Blue, Cabanne Course. No roads back in there. Just mule trails, a wagon trail to Mine a Breton. Coon-ass what they be called. I heard once it from a French word mean whore's child, trick baby. Another time it's French for easy pussy, skunk. Cause they mix-race.

"People say they descended from the French miners that Sir d'Reno left behind when the Mississippi Bubble bust in the time of Louie the Greatest. Then the French Indians with a white chief come and live by them in a Indian town, and they mix up together. Later on some Haitian slaves from the new plantations run off in the New Madrid earthquake and hide out at the old mines. And they be mixing up together too.

"Coon-asses grow they own vegetables, corn to cook whiskey, grapes to make wine. Fish in the rivers, game in the woods. They want a little cash money for ammunition, jeans, tobasco sauce, they just dig down about six foot to the lead ore. Wash it in the rocker box, take it down to the store by the smelter. They be poor. They dirty. Can't read or write. But they happy. They live off the land.

"Then along come this railroad. What did they want with a railroad? Suppose to go up the Forch a Reno to the big new deep shaft lead mine at Shibboleth. What the coon-ass be thinking they see this railroad and all them poor nigger and white immigrant working mens and womens . . . they think if they let the railroad in there, pretty soon they be wage slaves too. Laying track. Crawling around on they hands and knees in the mud in the dark a mile underground in the deep shaft at Shibboleth lead mine. St. Joe Lead Company got mineral rights to all the land, say go down in that deep shaft or you evicted.

"So when Mr. Jesse James and his brother Frank and their associates come along one night on extremely tired horses, they was welcome to stay among the coon-ass. Mr. James just had some difficulty making a withdrawal from the bank at Gallatin, Missouri, and found it necessary to shoot the cashier in the head. The travelers was most grateful for the hospitality of people who mind they own business so well that with Americans moving in around them since more than a hundred years, they still talking French. They don't hardly understand no English. What they talk together be old fashion poor people's French from the time of Louis the Greatest, mix with Indian French and Haitian nigger French. Can't none of them read or write. No roads up in there. No telegraph. Coon-ass be all family to each other, and they don't hardly have nothing to do with nobody outside they own community. A stranger come around asking questions, the word spread.

"My daddy was of the opinion the coon-ass showed the brothers where to rob the train out on the main line at Gad's Hill. Mr. Jesse and Mr. Frank gone through the cars saying, 'Let's see your hands, boys. We don't take the money off no honest working man with calluses on his hands. We just want the loot from the plug-hatted gentleman.' But the money they took from the express car safe be the payroll for the workers laying track on the Forch a Reno line.

"The Gad's Hill robbery I believe was prior to the experiment with a steam drill. Making up a whole extra payroll don't help the railroad profit-and-loss, and a piece of machinery, it keep on working whether you pay it or not.

"Now Big John like I say he not dumb, he just half smart. Naturally he thinking if the steam drill beat him, then the Captain he bring in steam drills and lay off mens. And the workingmens they see what be coming down. They saying, 'Go, John. Go! Beat that drill!'

"John striker name Loomis. He turn the drill rod a half turn, Big John hit it, BLAM!

"Bluff he drill in Loutre Bluff, that mean *otter*. Otter Bluff. Only it just one side of this round high ridge name Venner. River run around in a loop almost a island so one side Escarp d'Venner call Loutre Bluff, other side where the tunnel suppose to come out be Cuivre Bluff. Mean copper. Venner mean Venus in French or fucking and pussy-licking like lechery only not like there be anything wrong with it cause the Frenchmens and Frenchwomens, you know, has a different attitude.

"I once know a woman name Venus. She high yellow. Venus Pearl. Um-HMM! Work the Victorian Club on Cote Brilliant Avenue. Loot her, she quiver.

"This ridge he drilling in be the Venus Mound. Be from the

Mound People built a mound of the red earth in the shape of a woman there like the serpent mound in Ohio only this a woman you know between the legs and forty foots high and a hundred foots long. On top of this ridge be the Venus mound of the earth, and it was holy to the coon-ass. In the bluff below the Venus Mound be a cave call the Venus Cavern, a deep winding motherfucker of a cave with side passages and rooms and underground lakes. Got blind white fishes and blind crawdads in the underground lakes and springs, and white watercress growing in the spring. And on the walls deep in the underground rooms be pictures cut in the stone and painted on from the ancient Indians from before there was even white men, the Bluff People not Indians more like . . . well, they was cave mens.

"So the coon-ass discover this Venus Cavern and it was the first place they live and hide out and they see the writing on the wall. It be writing in pictures call petro . . . petroglimpse. The sacred writing in the stone. The writing on the wall they study by the firelight, by lantern light. Some bc frogs . . . salamanders . . . . Some pictures be of the animals they hunt, deers and buffalos and wild pigs and hairy elephants . . . . My great-grandaddy say some was pictures of mens and womens you know doing it. Every which way. So they call it Escarp d'Venus cause Venus the goddess of love. I mean every which way. Orgies, man. People call the Venus Cavern Cunt of the World. Cunt of the Earth.

"Some of them be Tamarora Indians that live by the Great Mound by Cahokia at East St. Louis, be Mound People. They the most ancientest Indian tribe still not extinct when white mens come, say, in Indian language, that be the Cunt of the Earth. And when the war god Tashiva be come to love the earth, he cause the New Madrid earthquake. He come in the form of a giant pecker . . . a big black pecker big around as a freight car, long as a train, and he fuck old mother earth up her cunt in the Venus Mountain, and she shake—oh, she shake and quake, shake and bake. That be the New Madrid Earthquake. They felt it a thousand miles away in Pittsburgh and Charleston, South Carolina. That be the last the god come into time, into white mens time. Be 1811 white mens time he last fuck the earth, I mean love her.

"And now come the white mens to drill a tunnel, lay steel track, and a steam drill into Venus Mountain, Cunt of the Earth. I mean the vagina. That a softer word, man. You know what I mean? So they come with steel drills, hammering, and dynamite.

"Loomis, big John striker, he have a way he talk to John, help keep his rhythm. I mean he had the heft in he strong back, and Loomis he talk sweet shit to him, 'Rock's a young girl, fuck her easy, Big John, ease it in. She love you, man . . . she helping . . . . She want it in her. She love you, man . . . she helping . . . . She want it in her, she want you inside, slow and easy . . . smooth, man. You striking smooth.'

"And beside him the steam drill going, 'Whoosh-puht . . BLAM! . . . whoosh-puht . . . BLAM!'

"Big John he only half smart but he was, well, he was a splendid athlete. Like you black athletic stars today, half smart and very good at playing boys' games for the white TV, gladiators. Big John he a Uncle Tom gladiator, and he hit smooth. He hit smooth and easy right on time. Right on. He don't waste no motion or crab the drill. He ease it in so the mountain taking it up inside her. Like I learned once myself working in a factory making aluminum window frames, and you use these self-tapping iron screws and put beeswax on, and the pilot hole be smaller than the shank of the screw, so you put just the point in with tap grooves, and you screw it in. You cut you own thread in the aluminum . . . . I be young then, a young soldier, and the Time Study Man he be there, his clipboard and pocket watch, so I trying too hard, see, drop the screw on the floor, screw it in sideways. And this other dude name Henry—his name be Henry—he show me how. 'Like a young girl, see . . . . Be gentle at first, see, go in a turn till it stick, back off a half turn, go in a turn till it stick, back off a half turn, go in a turn or two, back off, then you go in easy . . . smooth . . . all the way . . . right down to the nitty gritty smooth.'

"Big John, that how he drill into the stone, that soft limestone of the mountain. He *love* his drill rod in . . . .

"But the steam drill always breaking down. It go a while, 'Whoosh-puht . . . BLAM! . . . whoosh-puht . . . BLAM! . . . whoosh-puht . . . ' and break down. Professor Owen he get red in the face and holler at the dirty-face white boy Kempf, 'Do this . . . do that,' and the boy saying, 'I already did,' and sometime almost crying, the Professor abused him so in front of everybody.

"What they doing to the mountain . . . to the earth . . . the stone cry out. It making these noises like you rub flesh off bones, a screaming of the steam drill against the live . . . that stone, limestone of the earth.

"Coon-ass hillbillies watching, some be friends of Big John. Call him Fort John and John l' Fort. Mean strong. One friend to Fort John be a old half-Choctaw eat snuff name Gross Vase, like to spit on the ground close by the captains, and one time he hit Captain Hoyt's boot. Captain say, 'I'll have you horse-whipped!'

"Now Gross Vase don't understand English. Don't hardly none of the coon-ass understand it. They old languages Choctaw, Abenaki, Puant and African be all forgot. What they talk together be just ignorant poor people's French. But Gross Vase understand enough.

He know he being insulted. And he turn around, push his pants down showing his mean red ass and he say, 'Pupp-up-put-up-pp . . . !' You know the sound I mean.

"Captain Hoyt he stop, think a minute. People gathered around. He say, 'You get off the Railroad property!' Hoyt be a young dude, handsome, blond hair, blue eyes, short hair plastered with sweat down against his skull. He a ladies' man, talk up the young working womens. And he know some of them too. He maybe thirty years old. Say, 'You're trespassing.'

"Old Gross Vase he brown in the face like leather, barrel chested. He built like a barrel, like a boar hog up on its hind legs and he wear a black wide-brim Indian hat. Look like he ready to tear into Captain Hoyt. He thinking. Some workingmens gathered around, a few of the coon-ass. More of them up the side of the bluff. And always there be the coon-ass hillbillies up on the rim of the bluffs watching, carrying lever-action Winchesters and old trapdoor Springfields. Now one of them take a potshot. BLAM! Kick up some dust and rocks.

"Gross Vase he rub his hands together once, hold them up like he getting ready to fight. Captain Hoyt he have that big old forty-four revolver strap on his leg, his right hand rest on the butt. Gross Vase tuck his arms across his chest like Sitting Bull kind of laughing to heself and he say . . . he look the Captain in the eye and he stand there like a big old razorback hog up on he hind legs, a sawed-off oak tree he roots in the ground and he say . . . he don't turn around this time. Gross Vase a famous storyteller among the coon-ass, a raconteur. He a master of rap cause he can, well, his name is cause he can talk out both ends of his body. Any time. And he say to the Captain, 'Ppp-up-up-up—upppp—ppp-ip-pp!'

"Captain Hoyt look at him kind of funny like he wonder if there be some trick to it. People be laughing, giggling, snickering. They smirk, poke each other, laugh at the Captain. And he don't like that much. He turn dark red in the face all down his throat and back of the neck. He rest his hand on the butt of that big old forty-four.

"Gross Vase move his head a certain way, and BLAM! A shot from the rim high up in the cedars on the bluff spray chat on the ground about three inches behind the Captain's heel. He jump up in the air, squeal like a girl. Then he hauling at his old gun. Only it stuck in the holster. And workingmens around smile.

"Big John he thinking fast. There be some people killed in about another minute. He go up to Hoyt that quick, take his arm say real respectful, say, 'May I speak with you, Captain?' And he hold onto the white man arm with a gun on the end of it, move him, manhandle him but respectful and talking to him, and I don't know what he say.

But Gross Vase and the coon-ass with him down on the right-of-way, they gone.

"The coon-ass hillbillies and Gross Vase, they know Fort John. And he tell lies to them and sing songs. He sing,

Ain't no hammer in this mountain
Ring like mine . . . .

He sing about when he a little baby on his momma tit, and he take a hammer

And a little bitty nail . . . .
Drive it in my daddy's knee.

You heard something like this story before, but I am telling you how it was.

"Now the coon-ass be gambling people. Lay down on a horse race, a cock fight, a flea circus. Bet on the weather, and on a man against the machine. Most of the workingmens and womens—black and white, Chinamens and Swedes and Polish and Italians—they put money down too. Even coon-ass got money on the steam drill be yelling for Fort John as the sun go down.

"He straining. He know to pace hisself at the hard labor. Even *half* smart he know a better steam drill coming, and a better drill after that. No way the working man going to win over the machine. He just being a fool. Only all them yelling for him and put they money down, and even they put money down against him be yelling for him too. They want a hero. You be a hero, pays the price. You pay in time. They take time off you life. He don't have to strain to be at the drill. He just work natural all day, he would have beat the drill. Only he never know for sure. All them yelling, 'Big John . . . Fort John . . . " You stop living for you self.

"They agree the contest going to . . . it was just a try-out at first but along the way it was . . . it become a contest, and they agree it end at eight by Captain Hoyt's gold pocket watch, he railroad watch. High summer time in August, that a half hour after the sun go down over the bluff to the west above the Forch a Reno and light still high in the sky, the Captain he hold up his old .44 Colt pistol and BLAM! The contest was over. And they turn off the steam drill, and Big John lay down his hammer and they measure. That steam drill had cut twenty-nine feet into the limestone.

"And Big John, he drill forty-one.

"And all the working mens, and the strong working womens, and the whore womens, and the coon-ass, they cheering, yelling, dancing around by the fire light. And Mr. Jesse and Mr. Frank James and associates was passing through and if there was one thing they hated besides Pinkerton detectives and banks, it was the railroad—trying to make everybody live by railroad time. They join in too. Coon-ass shoot off they guns up on the bluff side and build the bonfires, and music start again, and dancing. I mean they party down, see. They partying all night long.

"Only Big John take a stitch in he side. And Mary Ann his tall woman, she come and she put her arm around his waist, and he drop his hammer, and he lean on her walking back down the track to his crib in a old dirty white miner's tent. And a little boy he pick up the hammer like it was holy, like Joe Louis' nine-ounce gloves, and he follow down the tracks and more of the childrens following.

"Fort John sit down on the tick mattress, and he ask for some that white whiskey. And Gross Vase he give him a jar of the good corn. John he take a long drink and he laid back and holding Mary Ann by the hand, and he died. He lay back with a smile of . . . like a statue . . . and he died.

"And they stop the clock and turn the mirror to the wall and they take off his work clothes. And Mary Ann herself the tears run down her face, she wearing a blue dress, has blue eyes, almost white, a tall woman, and long dark hair . . . the most beautifulest woman in Missouri, my grandaddy say. Her mother a house servant to Governor Marmaduke, the tears run down her face like from a deep spring in the earth. She wash his fine brown body, and wash off the sweat from his brown skin, and they dress him in his blue trousers and white shirt, and laid two big Indian head pennies on his eyes.

"And the word go out to the working mens and the coon-ass, and the music and the dancing stop. And a hush fall over the whole railroad camp, over three hundred mens, and womens, and childrens of all colors and all places of the earth. And they come in a long slow line one by one to pay they respects by the lantern light, filing one by one past the body of big John laid out . . . and the only sound be the whippoorwills going 'Whippoor-WILL . . . whippoor-WILL . . .' as they come in that long slow line by the lantern light.

"Loomis and another man making the coffin. Make it from the wood they borrow from the steam drill crates. Bring and set it down by Big John in the lantern light.

"In the morning was the funeral, this holy roller preacher before sunrise so it don't cut into the work day, and Captain Hoyt and Professor Owens and Kempf.

"Only something was wrong.

"Just a few of the workingmens and womens come to the grave on a shelf of the rocky ground by the greenblue river under a cypress tree.

"Most of the working mens and womens and all the coon-ass be gone. Left out of there in the night. Cause they know what be coming down for steam-drilling the Cunt of the Earth. Mary Ann be gone. And Fort John' little boy John Henry Junior left out of there in the night.

"My great-grandfather was John Henry l'Fort. John Henry Stokes. My grandfather be his son. Most all the black prisoners in the jails and state pens . . . and poor white workingmens too . . . be childrens of John Henry. Understand? Got nothing left to be but criminals. You so educated, think about it.

"And all the white mens, the Captains, the Professor and the pimple face boy, the hillbilly preacher, and a few Uncle Tom workingmens and whore womens, they all that be there, only twenty or so people as the sun come up, and the Captain look around. He be nervous, the silence, the working mens and womens gone in the night. Not even the birds singing.

"And just before the sun come up over the ridge to shine on the blue limestone of the Forch a Reno bluff . . . there be a slow shaking of the earth . . . like it was waves on the water, only through the land like the land was made of jelly, and the rocks—like the earth be jello—it was waves from the south, from New Madrid. Only at the same time, flame come flashing out of the tunnel mouth and up on the bluff side above the tracks. And rock commenced to crumble, and the whole side of the bluff—huge motherfucker blocks of the golden limestone come down, and the tunnel falling in. The sound THUMP hit you in the chest, the explosion of all the dynamite at once that over the last three months the coon-ass had stole. I mean it was a *ton* of dynamite. Be like Sampson push apart the pillars of the Temple and the Temple falling down.

"They just buried the tunnel, and a quarter mile of track . . . dammed up the Forch a Reno and made a lake. And the Captains, the Professer, the Holy Roller Preacher—all the white mens and the steam drill buried under that whole mountainside of rock . . . .

Hey bo ben
This story en'."

Croppers on the Highway

This is another story that was told to me by old M.D. Stokes at the Missouri State Penitentiary in Jefferson City. "The croppers on the highway?" he said. "I be fifteen years old.

"White boys one of them Mr. Matthews son J.T. come around shoot tin cans off the fence post childrens playing nearby. Be at Sweet Home Church the fourth place they move us to not a mile from where Mr. R.C. Matthews evict us from in the first place.

"That be in the Depression. Mens out of work. Womens offer it to get food for they childrens. President Roosevelt giving the parity to the farmer so he don't plant so much. Only the farmer Squire Houck suppose to pay half to the cropper and a quarter to the tenant Mr. Matthews just like it was cotton. Farmer and the tenant put they heads together say all right, we don't use croppers no more just day labor, and they keep all that parity for theyself.

"Buy tractors. Don't need us no more. Or mules.

"Papa go to Mr. Matthews ask him, 'Did my parity come yet?' Mr. Matthews he say no, not yet. Papa go three times ask for he check. Mr. Matthews lie deny him three times say it never come. Papa go to the courthouse. They say the checks all gone out. He go to Mr. Matthews again say what they told him and he be thinking he write a letter to Mr. Henry Wallace.

"'Why, Mr. Johnson,' old Matthews say, 'I don't believe you can write your name.'

"'My boy can.' Papa put his hand on my shoulder.

"Matthews say, 'Oh no, you don't want to write to that sonofabitch.' He hem and haw go mess around in the pigeon holes over he desk, come up with a envelope, say 'Why here's one . . . must have overlooked it.'

"Give Papa the check say he appreciate he not tell anybody or all the croppers be asking.

"Like it be punishment Mr. Matthews he put us off.

"Only all around the cotton fields in the Swamp East be happening the same thing come lease day January 10th. Croppers be put off the land January 10th.

"Reverend Whitfield see a Ford tractor big as a hay barn a coming to plow the peoples under the earth. Be asking, 'Where is that parity for us?' Say in the last meeting, 'Let us starve right out on the highway so the whole world can see.'

"Mrs. Roosevelt see our picture say what a pitiful sight all strung out on the road. Peoples stand around by theyself and in groups, mens, womens, boys and girls shivering in the cold, little childrens they bellies swole out cause they be starving, babies crying, bed sheets, old clothes, chester drawers, bed springs scattered on the ground. She send us army tents.

"State Police come to inspect us with a old prison doctor he hand shake, say we a health hazard. Got no decent water. We shit where we eat. What they has to do is clear us off the public highway and place us in camps so we can be vaccinated against the diseases.

"Come in seventeen highway department trucks. Say we all has to move to the other side of the road, and they search our plunder. Papa have a little .410 he shoot rabbits for the pot. Be confiscated.

"They separate us white from black, order us into the trucks.

"That how they do. Take you guns, load you in the truck to the concentration camp. Be in a swamp on the floodway. Call it Nowhere Junction. Police watching us, don't let peoples in or out.

"Governor say the army tents be lost. Keep on moving us so we don't be there when peoples wants to help. Move us to a old dance hall in New Madrid, to out behind the levee at Dorena, to some cropper cabins on the plantation that the old woman died and heirs be suing. Say we give a black eye to the Show Me State, the show-me-the-color-of-you-money . . . that fine old slave state of Missouri. Governor say we doing this cause we be promise a Collective Farm like LaForge. He the Timber King log 10,000 acres, sell it off.

"He planter friends don't want nobody to help us. Tell the Red Cross keep they hands off cause Union Agitators calling our tune. Wants us to starve and suffer the misery until we come back to them for day labor fifty cents a day.

"They move us again to Sweet Home Church more than a hundred peoples trying to live in a little one-room country church. We make tents from old quilts and sheets, sleep on the floor between the pews. We have a outhouse to the church only before long it overflowing. Peoples get sick from the flux and grippe.

"Squire Houck owner of the church land sue the deacons for allowing us there. Trying to sue us off.

"I say, 'J.T., be childrens where you shooting at.'

'It's only a beebee gun,' he say.

'Put you eye out.'

"Use to J.T. and his older brother William and me was best friends. William he interested in the Indian mounds, collect arrow heads, what he call celts you plow up in the fields. Our hideout be on a Indian mound with trees and brush growing up out of it. We dig down to make our fort to some big old flag stones. Lift them off, dig some more, we find a skeleton. Don't tell nobody cause William he say be against the law to dig up a skeleton. Say it must be a man that was killed cause he all scrunched up knees to he chin, and we suspects.

"William have a Red Ryder beebee gun from the Sears Roebuck. We shoot tin cans, birds, pictures from the wish book. I bring William a arrowhead, he allow me to shoot Red Ryder. I take a interest.

"Only J.T. don't like it I always be bringing arrowheads to he brother and once he call my sister Josephine out of her name. I lay one up side J.T. head he holler. William ain't no never mind to him. J.T. he don't forget neither I whip him good.

"Sometime Josephine run with us, sometime other cropper childrens. Mr. Matthews he farm a quarter section, plow forty acres hisself, have three cropper families. All us childrens run together sometime, but mostly William, me, and J.T.

"J.T. say, 'You trespassing.'

"'We use to be friends.'

"' . . . Got us a Ford tractor.'

"'Act like you forgot my name.'

"'Called my pappa a thief!'

"He lever the gun, take a shot at a bird on the fence. Bluebird fly off.

"That where we at when the sorority girls come.

"First be the black professor have his own automobile. Get out with a camera to take our picture.

"Papa go up to him say, 'We tired of you all taking our picture.' Say, 'I be Walter Johnson leader of the Sweet Home Church group, and you will not take our picture here.' He say we tired of our picture in the newspaper our picture in the magazine and nobody nowhere to help, except Mrs. Roosevelt and they lied to her and lost her tents. Not even the Red Cross. Say CIO be involved and we not a disaster cause we brought it on ourself. Papa say, 'You all making black fools of us!'

"We sure enough a raggedy ass sight—blanket over a clothesline for a tent, lean-tos made out of old boards, burlap, cardboard, pieces of tin roof, womens cook by the fires or just trying to stay warm, childrens mope around too hungry to play or act up.

"Professor Langston he disturbed. He look around like he a explorer in darkest Africa, we the starving natives in the bush. 'Mr. Johnson, what do you need?' he ask.

"Papa say, 'I requires a lease, a crib to stay in.'

"'What do you need most?' Professor Langston ask.

"'We needs food. Childrens here be starving. We needs food, shelter, clothes to keep warm, and medicines the most.'

"Professor say, 'My only object in taking the pictures would be to acquaint people in Jefferson City with the wretched condition of the share croppers . . . to move them to secure for you some of the things you so badly need.'

"'We don't study no more picture taking,' Papa say.

"'But pictures would substantiate my appeal for help. They would tell your story far more eloquently than anything I could say.'

"Papa hear that before, from white men. He look around the church yard and off across the bare fields. He look over at Mama and take a deep breath, then at me.

"'With your permission, Mr. Johnson,' the Professor say.

"'We hard-working mens and womens be evicted from the plantations,' Papa say. 'They lying about us, say we lazy shiftless vagrant niggers wants the Government to pay us and not do no work.'

"Professor Langston say he understand that.

"He go around, Papa introduce him, talk to peoples, take they picture. He a young dark brown man dress like a preacher in a white shirt not half so stout as Papa. He write down you name when he take you picture, listen to what you say.

"He take a picture of a barn door leaned up against the side of the church, woman set on a crate giving suck to her baby. Another picture be a dog watching over two childrens asleep on a mattress on the ground. One be peoples kneeling where they throw straw down in the church yard praying, little childrens with swole out bellies stand among them, look you in the eye.

"Professor Langston thank Papa and left, and that all we see of him for a month.

"Then he come back with two sorority girls, Miss Adele James the Basileus of the Delta Sigma Theta and Miss Cynthia Bolt of the Alpha Kappa Alpha, who also be president of the Lincoln University Student Council. Miss James later she say Professor Langston when he return tell her American civilization class about us. She want to know if we ask about her and her friends, and he say yes and he answer she and her friends not interested in us cause they too busy thinking about the spring prom.

"Her and her friends went to prove him wrong. Take the money they save for they prom and collect money and clothes and all. They has to rent a big old rickity cotton trailer fasten on behind to Professor

Langston little Ford roadster to bring it all to us.

"They bring food, all kinds of clothes—hats, dresses, shoes, skirts, stockings, trousers, underwear, suits. Bring bags of flour, sugar, salt, oatmeal, rice and beans, can milk for babies, cod liver oil, and almost sixty-five dollars left over they give to us.

"I be the onliest one can read and write good so Papa have me write the letter of thanks for him.

Miss Bolt, Words cannot express how glad we was in having you young ladies and the Professor in our midst. I pray that you all arrive home safely. The money you give us was so much help and have been spent for what you all given it for. I bought $62.49 groceries and 6 cent stamps plus 17 cents the bus fare to Charleston add to $62.66. Balance in hand 5 cent. We think kind of you and pray for you success. From the Sweet Home group.

Walter Johnson.

"Miss Bolt and Miss James gather the childrens together for school, give the elocution lesson and spelling tests. I be a freshman in the high school assist them in every way.

"Miss Adele James encourage my literary efforts. I write her a poem go like this:

The Negro

He plow from six to six at night
Without a single thing to bite.
His head and feet be wrecked in pain,
He sit and listen to the Boss explain.

The Negro was freed from acting the slave

By a very tall man the name of Abe.

"Miss Adele James she a fox. Walk with me down the path, teach me to French kiss.

"I tell her, 'White boys disrespect my sister.'

"'She is a beautiful young lady,' say Miss Adele James. 'She my ideal of Cleopatra Queen of the Nile.'

"'Name Josephine.'

"'When she prepared, she must come on to Lincoln. Pledge Alpha.'

"'We raggedy ass cropper peoples a long way from that, Miss Adele.'

"'You think we so different? Daddy be a mail man, Mama have her a beauty shop.'

"'That boy J.T. I whip him good. He never forget.'

"'Put the past behind you, Cecil.'

"I say, 'It be on my mind. He spy on her when she go to do her business.'

"'This happening to you-all be hard. Be sad and pathetic. But suppose you a farmer?'

"'Since I seven years old I do farm work—pick cotton, chop cotton.'

"She say Professor Langston lecture the civilization class about us. 'Suppose you be the farmer. Government give you a Ford tractor. Just hand it to you. Now you don't need croppers.'

"'Or mules.'

"'Don't pity youself, Cecil. Be a man.'

"'That parity suppose to be for us. Mr. Matthews stole it.'

"'We *had* this argument.'

"'Yes, m'am.'

"'Don't say *m'am* to me.'

"We sitting on a cypress log by the drainage ditch. I look at her.

"She kiss me. 'Put the past behind you, Cecil,' she say. 'Live.'"

"Cross burn in the stubble field. Next night a cross burning off across the road. Papa say meaning of the burning cross be you burn charity out of you heart.

"Got to where you can't use that outhouse no more, people go up the ditch in the woods do they business. J.T. and he friends lurk about, spy on the womens. Catch Josephine by herself all cramped up from the flux, take her off, three, four white boys. None of the womens tell me cause they afraid what I do.

"Then Papa have a letter from Professor Langston say black peoples in St. Louis and Reverend Whitfield and the Scarlet Bishop contrive to obtain us some land. Say they find 90 acres south from Popular Bluff at three and a quarter per acre, come to three hundred dollars. Down payment be fifty dollars. Say he gone to St. Louis with Miss Adele James of the Alpha Kappa Alpha sorority, and they decide the $31.00 additional they collect for food and medicine for us can go to the down payment. Reverend Whitfield say he the one persuade us to camp on the highway in the first place he make up the rest from his own pocket. Left barely enough for he family to eat.

"So we move onto Hard Scrabble up among the hillbillies in the

Ozarks, only we know to farm in the black dirt bottomland. Don't have no mule or plow even we could plow in that flinty ground, red brown from all the iron in it like dry blood. That be hillbilly land. Black peoples die on it.

"I write to Professor Langston for Papa,

> *You know we are out here in the hills and rocks. We can't farm and the white people doesn't hire no labor and if we don't get grant checks, I don't know what become of us.*

"I have a ideal what J.T. and them done to my sister be sure when I see her puke. Say I go back hide in the woods tend to business with J.T. Matthews lay for him clip him up side the head, cut his throat.

"Josephine cry Mama be crying Auntie Rue all the womens has to pray on me. Old time country niggers they pray you down turn the other cheek.

"Josephine stay by me watch when I try to run off. I go down in the weeds and willows by the clear creek under the bridge she waiting on the other side. She take my hand say, 'Cecil, be my business.'

"I ask her, 'You my sister?'

"'They put you *away*.'

"'Think I lay around wait for police?'

"'Hurt a white boy you be lynched.'

"'Got to catch me first.'

"'Crackers take it for they excuse, burn us all out.'

She trying to shame me.

"'Set they dogs on us.'

"I left on out of there, lie about my age, join the Merchant Marines.

"While I gone Papa move up to St. Louis sweep floors in the small arms plant. Josephine have her trick baby go on the welfare. After the war they be staying in the Pruitt Igoe projects.

"Tell that to Mrs. Roosevelt. You write it down."

Deer in June

I cater to city men, but that boy . . . always talking about the stock car races at St. Louis. I will tell you the truth. He is in the penitentiary.

He lasted about a week as kitchen help at the lodge over to Lake Ozark, and Henry had to let him go from pumping gas. His pappa was Naman Ralls that fell down drunk in a charcoal rick and burned to death, and the boy the sole support for his mama and four little ones. I was naturally sorry and hired him on.

His last trip with me, our sport was in advertising. Name of Sweringen, and he had brought his little girlfriend. Some I care for, some I don't. Either way I get my money, and now and then one like the brewing fellow will give me a nice tip.

Mr. Alec Sweringen, he did not leave us a tip.

I don't blame him.

When we met them at Eden park the boy had his shirt off. He was leaning against the fender of the truck there fooling with his twenty-two rifle, his stomach hanging out over his motorcycle belt with all the studs and reflectors on it.

They come in one of them little foreign cars, and Mr. Alec Sweringen he was wearing a red sport shirt with big white flowers all over, red swim trunks, and tennis shoes without no socks. He was somewhat stout, had a young face and long gray hair, and wore black rim eyeglasses and smoked the little cigars.

The girl I seen her kind before, in magazines and on the television. She had on gold sandals and like a little white night shirt you could see through and under that a yellow swim suit that covered her teats and the hair between her legs and not an inch more. I would never allow a woman of mine to walk around like that.

You can tell by how they are dressed. I always say, if you want to know how to dress on a float trip, wear a long sleeve shirt and something on your feet. I wear a long sleeve gray homespun shirt, bib overalls, a visor policeman's cap to keep the sun off, and solid high top shoes. My name is John Count. I been a Gasconade River float trip guide for seventeen years.

I and the boy loaded the twenty-foot john boats and the Mercury outboard motor and the commissary chests and the tent and all the equipment into the flat bed truck, and the boy rode in back. The boats are the shape of the Indian dugouts but made of ash lumber. The Frenchmen who come for the lead mines long ago called them pirogues, and in my great-grandfather's time they was used to float iron down from the smelter at St. James to make the Union ironclads at Carondelet.

We drove by old 66 and over the ridge to put in at Adam Ford. The girl throwed her little gold sandals up in the front end of the fishing boat and waded out and climbed in. I tried to tell her, "They's sharp rocks on the bottom, and broken glass and old tin cans too."

She tossed her long straight hair and bugged out her yellow eyes at me and says, "I've got tough feet."

Then the boy taken out in the commissary boat like the drag races and if it was wheels and concrete instead of the ten-horse outboard and river water, he would have left a path of burning rubber a quarter mile long.

"Cantrell Bluff!" I hollered after him.

"Yeah . . . yeah . . . yeah!" he hollered back, waving his arm like he was at the rodeo on top of the Brahma bull. Sometimes the first stop is Cantrell Bluff, sometimes Purdue Creek.

I got my party set up with live minnows in the long hole at Straight Bluff. Sweringen knowed which end of the rod was which but he spent half the time putting new minnows on the hook for the girlfriend and that's what he was doing when he got a nice strike, and lost it. Pretty soon she was bored fishing and took off that night shirt and just laid up in the front of the boat all but naked taking a sun bath.

She was still laid out like that when we swung in for lunch. The boy come wading out and grabbed the bow chain and pulled us up onto the gravel bar. She made him take her hand to help her out, and he hung his head sideways at her, and I could see it from where I was at he nearly popped his jeans getting a hard on big as a horse. She saw it too. That's her trade, if you ask me.

In the afternoon Sweringen caught a few little line-side bass which anyhow is the best eating size, and when we pulled out for the night at Azure Spring I cooked them up for supper.

A man that age should know to watch his liquor.

He offered and I taken a good long shot but when he offered to the boy I said, "That boy ain't but seventeen years old," and would not allow him to have none.

From where he was sitting on the bedroll on the other side of the fire, that boy's close-together eyes stared at me like two side-by-side shotgun barrels. Then he looked acrosst at the bluff and run his fingers through his long greasy tow hair, and he got up and fooled in his duffel bag by the water and went off along the bar out of sight among the willows.

"How do you like that whiskey?" Sweringen asked.

"Smooth as silk," I said.

"It's one of my accounts," he said. You'd think he laid an egg he was so proud. "Say, Deb," he said, "I could work him into a campaign."

Her model name was Deb Arnette. She was a home girl herself once upon a time. She smiled at me, and I know I seen her selling toothpaste.

"For sugar whiskey," I said.

"What's that?" Sweringen asked.

"This here is good for sugar whiskey," I said, "but it ain't the real corn."

He said, "It's charcoal mellowed."

I allowed that charcoal would take the edge off, but for the real thing you need malted corn. He never heard of malting, and there he was making up the advertisements for a whiskey company. He wanted to know all about it, so I told him how you throw a quart of shelled corn in each burlap sack and then you bury the sacks in a damp place about four inches deep and pile on dead leaves and horse manure, and with warm weather in ten days you dig it up, and the corn is sprouted. It changes from starch to malt sugar, and then you run that malted corn through the regular way. All the whiskey you buy in the store is just cane sugar and corn syrup and yeast.

"I prefer wine," said the girl.

You could hear the boy down the river shooting his twenty-two rifle at tin cans and bottles. That was reason enough right there not to hire him along on no more float trips. It don't make you less of a man to respect your customer. They come down here and pay a good price for their pleasure, not to watch you take yours.

He come back after a while and the girl asked him, "You kill any bears?"

"Ain't no bears," he said. "Just wild hogs."

"Are you serious?" she asked.

Sweringen laughed.

"What's so funny?" she asked.

"I thought you knew all about hogs," said Sweringen.

"We kept them in pens," she said.

I told him before not to talk about the wild hogs. I said it was time to go across and get the water. The sun was just gone down but still shining golden on the hickories and oaks on top of the bluff and the blue and gray and yellow limestone. Then the girl wanted to come along too, then both of them.

We climbed into the boat and drifted over where the clear blue water from the spring flows out into the chalky green Gasconade and landed on the bar just below it, and the boy wrapped the chain around a giant sycamore root. We taken the jugs and went up the path, the spring run twenty foot across and six foot deep, the watercress and pebbles on the bottom showing like it was crystal. We walked about a quarter mile up a little bay into the hundred foot limestone bluffs that rose above us with cedars and post oak in the niches and crannies, and the alder and witch hazel and boxwood on the shelf to either side of the water. The path turned sharp right, and all of a sudden there we was at the pool.

They stood there holding hands until she pulled her hand away.

The pool is maybe fifty foot across, the water pouring, bubbling in a deep limestone bowl out of a cave mouth forty foot down, clear blue, and the moss-grown limestone curving around the sides of it up to the fringe of trees getting just the very last gold of the sun now and the darkening blue sky above. They say the Indians had a name for it that meant the Eye of the World, but we call it Azure Spring.

Then the boy had to go up the dim path around to the side saying, "They's a dry cave up here." The girl, then Sweringen had to follow, and so I did. It was along a shelf of clay and rock chips to an opening behind two cedars, down in, then a straight dry cave stoop height and ten foot wide by forty long, with a little crawl passage from the back end. The bottom was covered with clean dry straw that somebody had took considerable trouble to haul in there. The boy looked proud and bashful and like he was daring me to stop him.

They was a empty pack of book matches, a torn shirtwaist, and something else by the wall just inside, and I saw her looking at it.

" . . . A trysting cave," said Sweringen.

"It's nice and cool," she said. "Can we stay here tonight?"

Sweringen looked at me.

"I surely wouldn't," I said.

"Why not?" she asked.

I looked at him, and then I said, " . . . Snakes, falling rocks, and in a cloudburst water could pour right through it."

We went back across the river with the filled jugs and I set a trot line and me and the boy pulled the boats up on the bar. It was a hot hazy evening the end of June, a mosquito whining around now and then, the frogs, and then the loud frantic whippoorwills over and over until they become the sound of the night.

The boy was down at the slough with his electric lantern shooting frogs.

Sweringen and the girl was sitting out in front of the tent by the last of the fire drinking that store whiskey, or he was. She had put on some jeans and a jersey top, cussing about the mosquitoes, and he had put on a gray sweatshirt. They said things to each other off and on.

At the time I could envy him that June-September romance, if only he knowed to watch his liquor. I laid out my bedroll down the other side of the boats on the gravel and stretched out. Mist was already forming and the few stars you could see was like from the bottom of the ocean.

He kept drinking, and they was arguing about something. I could hear her, "That's what you said before. You don't know what you want, Alec. You like things just the way they are."

"No . . . no . . . ," he said.

"You try to leave her . . . and she says she's going to commit suicide . . . and you put her in the hospital again . . . and then you feel terribly guilty . . . and you come back and tell me you can't do it yet."

"Just give me time, Deb . . . . I'm working things out."

"You are having your cake and eating it too as long as you can, and that's all . . . . . You use me to humiliate her, and as long as you stay with her I'm your little whore. I'm sick of it."

"That's a very hypocritical thing to say."

"Who the hell do you think you are, Alec? Are you—?"

"Now, look—"

"Are you worth two ordinary people? Two women?"

He made some smart answer.

Then she accused him of giving her the hair dye commercial just to get in her pants, and he asked where she would be if he didn't, and she said, "If I knew what was good for me, I'd go home to Wellsville."

Then they was quieter again.

She was north Missouri farm people, you see. Like most of the young ones now she had to go up to St. Louis to the big time. Some take to it, some don't.

I sat up out of the sound sleep, and I thought it was barn cats. But it was her, cussing. She come out of the pyramid tent in just her short yellow nightgown and went down by the water and sat there trying to light a cigarette.

Sweringen stuck his head out and called low to her.

She sat there not answering him, looking across the river, smoking, or like practicing smoking, looking tough.

You could hear him sigh, and his head went back inside, and he tossed around some, and then was still.

After a while the boy come up from the slough with his twenty-two and a mess of frogs as big as chickens all bloody and the entrails hanging out the way frogs will do when you use a hollow point.

He went right up to her and she did not act prissy the way city women would, and he stood there a while talking to her. Then he laid the rifle and the frogs down on the gravel and took off his belt, and his jeans and waded out into the water and dog paddled on across, and she peeled off the night gown and stood there a minute in the star light naked as the day she was born, and she waded out and swum after him, and through the mist I could barely see them coming out on the other side and go up the path along the run to Azure Spring and the cave.

The next day Sweringen was just plain sick. He vomited before breakfast and wouldn't eat nothing while we had the frog legs and some jack salmon and white bass from the trotline and cornbread, and all morning he just lay there in the middle of the boat wearing dark glasses not even pretending to fish and two or three times he leaned over to vomit, the last with dry heaves and passing some blood too so I was somewhat concerned about him. He took some weak tea and sugar and canned apricots at lunch though and seemed to keep that down.

Behind his back when she was coming from her weewee and she passed near the boy she taken his hand and pressed it to her cheek and kissed it, and Sweringen turned around in his dark glasses looking at them.

He wanted service. "Bring me this. Hand me that." It was not only because he was feeling poorly. He needed to let us all know in case we forgot how he was a pretty big fellow in the advertising.

I don't blame him.

It was at lunch time I started to hear the dogs. Someone's hounds was out chasing a deer.

I know about the notches in the stock of the boy's twenty-two rifle. They was twelve, for deer he took. Hunger knows no season. I might have done it myself now and again when I was a wild boy, and he had five to feed besides himself. This here is God's country to look at but mean to farm. Not everybody will go out of his way to tell the game warden if he sees a fellow dressing out a deer in June. Bearing tales is a good way to get your fences cut and your corn crib burnt. I keep my own counsel, but times is changing. This poor lovely land will pay if you save the deer and fish for guiding the city sports.

Just after we started again a green heron seemed like he saluted us with his harsh call, and I heard the dogs nearer. The commissary boat was still in sight when the little spike buck splashed into the water off the end of the gravel bar, looked back once toward the dogs, and commenced to thrash and then swim across like in a bad dream when you know they will kill you but you can only run slow.

The boy had all the time in the world. He cut the motor and rested his twenty-two on the truck piled in the center of the boat and fired three . . . four times, and the little deer jerked and squealed staining the clear green water red, and the boy drifted along and hauled it up into the boat.

"It's not deer season now is it?" asked Sweringen.

"Oh, mind your own business," said the girl. She had a bad sun burn and was wearing the jeans and a shirt.

But when we drifted nearer and the boy held up the carcass like he expected a loving cup, she was crying.

"No, it's not," I said.

"If I were a vindictive person," said Sweringen, "I'd report that boy."

He heard us too, and all of a sudden he weren't so cocky.

The fact is if I was alone and come on him doing like that, I might give him a piece of my mind. But I would not report him. Mr. Alec Sweringen, though, he just might.

And then I lose my guiding license.

Taking a deer from hunger is one thing. Poaching on a float trip in front of the sports, I can't abide that. When it's the boy or me, I have to think of my own young ones.

"You don't have to," I said, "because I'm reporting him to the Warden as soon as I can get to a telephone." And I did. "And after we pull out this evening and I pay him off," I said, "he is no longer employed by Count's Gasconade Float Trip Service."

He hung his head and started the motor on the commissary. Nobody else was going to hire him for the float trip guiding either.

The girl refused to leave with Mr. Alec Sweringen, and I was going to drive her to the bus at Waynesville. I did say she might have a while to wait in the dirty little station there with all the soldiers from Fort Leonard Wood. Then he begged her and she changed her mind, and they drove off in the little foreign car together.

That wild boy never was made for catering to city men. What he done was go up to St. Louis and rob the all-night markets.

Eight Ball

The last time I seen him he come straight from the gas station in his soiled work-shirt with his name on the pocket that he is so proud of. I got him a Stag beer and then I had to wait on some customers, and the next thing I know he is in a serious game of pool.

Chloe's new fellow Troy runs the table and studies his next shot. He has his sleeves tore off and likes to show his manly chest that ain't got a hair on it. He chalks his cue and points. " . . . Side pocket."

"Uhn-hunh," Walter says.

Chloe is barefoot setting at the end of the bar in her short shorts and a army T-shirt cut off to where they would arrest her for it on the street.

Troy shoots. Instead of kissing the 8-ball on the edge he knocks it pretty good and it drops all right, but in the corner pocket. He slams the butt of my $20 cue stick on the floor. "Shit!"

"Now you're coming with me," Walter says.

Chloe laughs.

Walter says, "You're laughing."

"Make it two out of three," Chloe says.

Troy asks her, "What are you trying to do, Chloe?"

Walter says, "Two out of three, three out of five, four out of seven. I'll whip his ass all night long."

Chloe shakes her head and laughs.

"You're just tormenting me."

I say, "That may be all she's got in mind, Walter." I look at him over the top of my eyeglasses.

Troy is racking the balls.

Walter stares at Chloe. "You said if I whip him at pool . . ."

"I said that?" She rests her hand on the baby laying asleep in my fiddle case.

Walter points at her with his cue stick and says to me, "She may be a whore but she ain't a liar."

Chloe says, "Walter always knew how to make me feel good about myself."

Troy tells Walter to watch his mouth, and Walter says he will whip his ass and ream it out. "Troy! . . . Walter! . . . You act civil!" I say. "Or I'm calling the Sheriff and lock the door."

Out the window screen behind them I see the swallows and purple martins chasing across the sky, and the rows of soybeans a half mile long to the cottonwoods on the bank of the river. Friday and Saturday nights cars and trucks is parked all around under the trees. People hang out drinking hard liquor and wine and passing a joint and send their kids in for cokes and six-packs. But Monday nights are slow and sometimes Little Bill or Tyree and them come in and we jam.

Walter lines up the cue ball, and breaks as hard as he can. Troy studies Walter, then the table, and takes his shot, and I think maybe it is going to be all right.

The only other customer now is this one old man and we get to talking and he says his name is Joe Maupin but everybody calls him Popeye, and his wife passed away recently.

"Scratch," Walter says.

"I know I scratched," says Troy.

Old Popeye says, "They're not playing for money?"

I say, "No, honey. For love."

Walter misses a shot and slams his cue down onto the table. Troy says, "How about if we just make this for five dollars?"

Walter says, "How about if I just stomp your shit?" Troy shuffles back a step.

"Walter!" Chloe says. "Rack the balls."

Walter stares at her with his neck bowed, then turns and racks the balls. Troy hangs back. "Break," Walter says. Troy moves to the table like Walter was a rattlesnake coiled up in the middle of it shaking his tail. "I ain't going to hurt you, sweetheart," Walter says.

Troy looks at Chloe, then at me.

"What you waiting for?" says Walter.

"This is bullshit," Troy says. He looks at me but I stay out of it. He looks again at Chloe. She shrugs and says, "Break." Troy's shot just kind of pats the balls on the shoulder and says excuse me. "That's a pussy break," says Walter. "It's legal," Troy says.

Walter lines up, and shoots like he was one of them old time knights on horseback and the cue stick was his spear and he was shoving it in Troy's asshole and up his spine and out the top of his head. The balls click and scatter every which way and I swear he knocked chips off of them.

Troy studies his next shot. He makes it and his next three, and parks the cue ball next to the side so Walter has to shoot near straight down on it to do himself any good.

Walter looks at it this way and looks at it that way and tries a fancy carom off the far end and knocks the 8-ball in out of turn. Oh how he curses and he swears and he takes and slams his cue stick down on the table and wraps his arms around his head like to make the world go away.

Chloe says, "Grow up, Walter."

" . . . I won the first game."

Chloe shrugs.

"You said."

"A woman has the right to change her mind."

Walter comes up close to Chloe. "We was together five years," he says. She says he never paid the child support. He says how can he pay child support in the penitentiary?

"I let you have my car," Chloe says.

"God damn little Jap car."

"It was all the property we ever owned."

Walter says don't talk to him about child support when he is in the penitentiary, and she put him there.

"When you beat me near to death . . . ," Chloe says.

"You ask for it—"

"And give me the concussion."

"Trolling around the taverns, bringing the baby."

"You threatened to kill the baby!"

"I never!"

" . . . And you expect me to leave here with you."

"You said—"

"Well I was bull-shitting."

Walter reaches out to take hold of Chloe. "I'll come with you any time I want."

She darts her long fingernails at his eyes, and he catches her wrists. I pull my cut-down baseball bat out from under the cash register and see Troy is edging toward the door. Chloe spits at Walter.

He flings her aside and falls against the bar, and rests there with his head bowed. After a while he says, "Get me a Blue Ribbon. One for him . . . and that guy too."

I say, "I ought to cut you off a hour ago."

Walter is fumbling with crumpled paper money. He lays out a bill. " . . . If you can act civil," I say. I fetch two cans of Blue Ribbon and one of Stag beer and open them. I take Walter's money and bring back change. "Her too," Walter says.

I move down opposite Chloe, but she shakes her head. I look her in the eye, say "Honey . . . ." Chloe shrugs. I open a can of Seven-Up and set it by her.

Walter is looking in his wallet. He takes out a worn piece of paper, unfolds it. He says, "I still have the one sweet letter that you wrote to me . . . in there."

Chloe catches my eye in the mirror behind the bar.

Walter says, "You forget in the penitentiary what it's like loving a woman."

"Love?" Chloe says.

"They try to make you be their woman. Tear your ass wide open."

"We know about that," I say. My nephew is in there yet, driving under the influence. He is Chloe's half-brother and their mother don't do nothing for him, so I am the one that sends him cookies and personal hygiene items. Chloe asks, "Walter, you seen Jackie in there?"

"Yeah I seen him."

Chloe says to Popeye, "He was railroaded."

I say, "Jackie was always the sweetest boy." His mother washed her hands of him.

Chloe says, "His lawyer didn't do shit."

"He sucks up to the Methodist chaplain's assistant."

I say, "I believe they open his mail."

"They ain't suppose to no more."

Troy has set down by Walter drinking his Stag beer. He says, "I hear weight lifting is big in there, any kind of body building."

Walter nods his head. "Only it ain't a real sport," he says. "It's a beef show."

Troy tries to talk with him about weight lifting and how to act in prison, like he was the young soldier asking the old soldier against the day he could wake up there his own self. He says, "I got no quarrel with you, Walter. You paid your debt."

"You better believe I did."

"Only Chloe's going with me now."

Walter tries to explain, " . . . Chloe and me was together five years. She had my little baby."

"We all know that. It was an important part of her life. But now she's going with me."

Chloe says, "I love it them talking about me like I wasn't here."

"They'll do that," I say.

"And they are going to decide everything about me, man-to-man."

"They will do that if you let them."

"Like I was the prize in a game of 8-ball pool."

"Honey, you did lead Walter to believe . . . "

"I'm tired of it."

Troy and Walter talk it over. Troy says, "I don't live there, Walter. But we spend time together." Walter says he don't blame her with him in the penitentiary. "Incarcerated. That's what the fancy niggers call it, you know. 'When I was incarcerated . . . '"

"You been out a while now, ain't you?"

"Sixty-one days."

"This is the first time you come around."

"I was getting on my feet."

"He is under a peace bond," Chloe says.

"Shit," Walter says. "You know . . . "

"I mean I can relate to your feeling," Troy says. "But things change."

"Me and that woman . . . I stand by her," Walter says.

"You a stand-by-your-woman man?" Chloe asks.

"In there . . . I would think over our times together one by one."

Chloe says, "It's almost like a song."

"She's laughing at me," says Walter.

Chloe sings, "If I had the wings of an angel, over these prison walls I would fly . . . "

"You all are laughing at me."

I say, "That's not so, Walter."

He fumbles at the snap of the sheath on his belt and lurches toward Chloe. "I'll teach her to laugh," he says. He pulls his folding knife, clicks the handle together, and shows the blade. "Go on, bitch. Laugh."

"You ain't told me nothing funny yet."

"Now you are coming with me, and we are going to talk," Walter says.

Chloe jerks back.

Troy eases himself out of the way behind the juke box.

"Walter . . . ," I say.

He stares at me.

"Get out."

"I never meant—"

"Get out," I say again.

Walter stares at me, then at Chloe, then moves toward the door. "You all are just laughing at me," he says. Popeye gets out of his way.

The baby is astir and whimpering and now he commences to cry. Chloe puts her hands to her breasts, lifts him out of the fiddle case, and moves to a chair facing the bar. Her nipple sticks out like the barrel of a gun. She pinches it and lets the baby fasten on with his little mouth.

Troy goes over to Chloe and stands just behind her watching. " . . . Little Walter," he says.

I say, "I knew him when he was not much bigger than that. I knew his mother."

"His mother still living?" Popeye asks.

I say in a home in town. Walter stays in her trailer on Perche Creek.

"What about his father?"

"He was a aircraft mechanic at McDonnell in St. Louis." We saw him now and then on the weekends. Then he just didn't come around no more.

His mother was the postmistress here in Vernal. We still had the P.O. then, in that little brick-block building with a porch and the windows all broke. She was kin to us, and Walter would play with Jackie and them. But one thing . . . he was a rock thrower. When Walter got provoked at you, he threw a rock. Once when him and Jackie was making a teepee out of a blanket, Walter decided it was just his Indian tent and told Jackie to go away. Jackie went away but then he concluded that wasn't right and come back because it was his Indian tent too. And Walter let fly with a rock. It hit Jackie in the forehead and it raised a lump big as an egg and it bled all down into his eyes.

Popeye says a boy like that needs a good whipping.

The baby has went to sleep. Chloe lays it in its blanket in the fiddle case.

Troy is over by the doorway. He says, "Uh, Lucille . . . "

"What?" I say.

"He's . . . right outside the door."

"Well, I'm not saying anything I wouldn't say to his face."

"He's like a shadow over me," Chloe says.

I move to where I can't exactly see him but I know he is there. "Walter . . . you go on home now," I say. "You had enough."

From the darkness he says, "I'm sorry I acted hateful."

"You should be."

"Please let me come back in."

"Not when you pull a knife. That is not allowed."

"I apologize. I'll give you my knife."

I ask, "Well . . . what do you all say?"

"Shit," Chloe says. "He still don't give me no space."

Walter says, "I bought you all a drink."

Troy says to me, "It's your place."

Chloe turns on the bar stool and puts her arms around him and rubs the small of his back. "Don't," Troy says. "He's watching."

I hold my peace.

Then I say to Walter, "Can you act civil?"

"Yes, Ma'm."

"And you will need to give me that knife."

Walter hands me the folded-up knife, then settles at the end of the bar by the doorway. Popeye gives him plenty of room.

I talk to him trying to keep him from looking at Chloe while she is putting on a show, petting Troy and pressing herself up against him. " . . . Don't rub his nose in it," Troy says.

"I love when you do that," Chloe says.

"What?"

"Rub your nose in it."

"Aw-w . . . "

"You scared of him?"

"I ain't scared of nobody, but he can stick that knife in your back."

"I think you're scared of him."

"He did hard time. You learn to stick a shiv in a man's back in there."

"Don't think about it."

Walter talks to Popeye. He says it hurts to see Chloe in here with some young guy. He understands though. He says, "She's a very good-looking woman, don't you think?" Popeye agrees. Walter says she can't help it the young guys come around and him incarcerated.

Popeye says, "Your mother was the postmistress?"

Walter shakes his head. "When I visit her at the home . . . she don't even recognize me."

"My wife was like that at the end."

Walter is in his cups. He sets there studying like he has to work a geometry problem in his mind. "The women these days . . . shit," he says. "I stand by my woman . . . only she lets me down."

"What do you think about that, Lucille?" Chloe asks.

I say, "I think Walter's wasting his time."

"That kid Troy," he says, "he don't mean no harm. But he's nothing."

I say, "Only if she don't see that . . . ?"

He says, "I'll make her see it. I'll wait until she sees it for herself."

"He drives a tractor for Bissonet."

" . . . I'm patient."

"He's kind of good-looking. He don't slap her around."

"You holding that up to me?"

"Face facts."

Walter stares out into the darkness.

"What was between you and her, it's over."

"My counselor in prison says it's very important for me to build a constructive relationship with a woman."

"That's a good idea, Walter, but—"

"The night they arrested me .... The reason I was drinking was I had a little dispute with Chloe."

"A little dispute?" Chloe says.

"The reason I had too much this evening . . ."

"Banged my head against the wall and give me the concussion."

"A fellow come in the station told me he seen my woman trolling in Lucille's place with some young guy."

Chloe says, "So it's my fault when he fucks up."

" . . . There's no reasoning with him," Troy says.

"I'm suppose to take him back because he needs me for his medicine."

"She has my little baby. See?"

"Once he threatened to kill my baby if I didn't take him back."

"Little Walter . . . ," Troy says.

"He is under a peace bond," says Chloe.

Walter says, "He knows me. His ears is—"

"He is on parole. If he comes within ten foot of my baby—"

"His little ears . . . "

"I will call the Sheriff. And he will be in the county jail tonight and back in the penitentiary next week!"

"His little ears is the same shape as mine."

"I'm not bullshitting!"

Walter sets there with his head bowed. He says, "That's my little son. And she drags him around to all the taverns."

"Now, Walter," I say, "that's ridiculous. In the first place, you rather she leave him home alone?"

"She done that too."

"And this here ain't hardly the East St. Louis night spots. Why, this place, it's more like the Vernal community center."

Popeye says, "I heard tell of some pretty good fights in this community center. And one man killed."

I say to Walter, "Chloe ain't your business no more."

His neck is bowed like he was fixing to come at me. He studies and says, "In the Book it is written—"

"What book is that?" Chloe asks.

" . . . Till death do us part."

"She don't see it that way."

"She will . . . "

I shake my head.

"I'm patient."

"It won't happen tonight, Walter."

"I'm patient as Job."

I study his face. ". . . If I give you back your knife, will you go home?"

Walter turns away from me. I seen tears in his eyes.

"Not tonight," I say.

"You throwing me out again?"

"As long as you act civil you are welcome in my place."

"I give you my knife."

"I got no complaint, Walter. I'm speaking as a friend of your mother. Go home, now."

"You cut me off and throwing me out."

"Now don't carry on."

"I been civil." To Popeye he says, "Ain't I been civil?"

The old man nods.

"He says so."

"It's time for everybody to go home," I say. "I'm closing. Troy . . . Chloe . . . it's closing time."

Walter holds out his hand. I give him back his knife, and he goes out into the darkness. I turn off the lights except a night light by the cash register. Chloe comes to the doorway holding the baby in its blanket in her arms.

At the end of the bar furthest from the door Troy says, "Where's he at?"

I say, "I told him to go home."

"You give him back his knife?" Troy asks.

"He's out there," Chloe says.

"Surely he will go home," I say. "He promised me."

Troy goes off to the men's room.

"He's laying in wait," Chloe says.

"He promised to go home if I give him his knife."

"His car's just setting there," Chloe says.

I say, ". . . Maybe he went for a walk."

"He's laying in wait out there," Chloe says. "He comes to my place in the night. I find where he's been setting under my window, cigarette butts in the grass."

I call, "Walter . . . ?"

Popeye says, "You think we should call the Sheriff's Department?"

"I hate to do that," I say, "with him on parole."

"Troy . . . ?" Chloe calls.

There is no answer.

Chloe truns around. "Where's Troy at?"

Popeye says, "The other fellow? . . . I believe he went to the men's room."

I call, "Walter! You go on home now."

Chloe is saying, "I wish he passed out. I wish he jumped in the river and drowned himself . . . I wish."

"You wish that?" I ask.

"Sometimes."

"Walter . . . !" I call out.

Popeye comes back from the men's room.

Chloe asks him, "Where's he at? Where's Troy?"

"Ain't nobody in there," Popeye says.

"Well . . . shit!" Chloe says.

"I believe he's gone."

"I am real tired of this."

"Just gone . . . out the window?" I ask.

"It don't have no screen," says Popeye. "The trash can was tipped over . . . ."

Chloe says, "I start seeing a guy, Walter scares him away."

"I'm surprised at Troy," I say.

"I have a right to my own life."

"I thought he had more sand."

"Walter scares them away. If he can't have me no more, nobody can. He's my dog in the manger."

"I believe I see him," Popeye says.

"What's he doing?"

"Setting on the picnic table whittling a stick."

"With his knife," Chloe says.

"Walter!" I say. "Put up that knife and go home now . . . You promised."

"Aunt Lucille, why did you give his knife back to him?"

"Honey, people and hogs act like you treat them. You take a chip of wood and scratch the dried mud out of the hair on Walter's back, he will grunt and wiggle . . . . You kick him in the ribs and fall down in the hog pen, he will tear your leg off."

"I already tried scratching his back."

"Walter . . . you go on home now. Hear . . . ?"

The old man says, "I think he's just going to wait until we come out."

"Will you go home if I play you "All the Pretty Little Horsies"?

From the darkness Walter says, "Aunt Lucille . . . messing with my mind."

When he was little and his mama and I visited together, he use to beg me to play "All the Pretty Little Horsies." I pick up my fiddle and tuck it under my chin. At the doorway into the darkness, I play,

Blacks and bays
Spotted and grays
All the pretty little horsies . . .

"He just sets there," Chloe says.

I say, "I know he is on parole . . . but I will have to call the Sheriff."

"Whittling . . . with his knife."

"I don't want to do this. I tried . . . " I go to the phone and dial.

"Here he comes," Popeye says.

I move to where I can see him get into his car.

The engine coughs once and stops. The starter runs again. Stops. It runs a long time, slows, stops; then kicks over once, barely turns, and dies.

Walter gets out. He has a tire iron in his hand. "God damn fucking no good little Jap car!" he says.

Chloe giggles.

Walter raises the tire iron at her. "I'll bust you wide open!"

We stare at him.

" . . . You all laughing at me."

You can hear again the distant horn of a towboat passing on the river, then the twittering of the purple martins.

He turns and kicks the car. "God damn fucking little Jap car anyhow!"

He smashes the windshield. Three, four times he smashes clean through, beats with his fists and smashes the glass with his tire iron. Then he flings it away into the field among the soybeans, clenches his bloody hands under his armpits, and walks off crying toward the river.

Chloe is huddled over her baby. She moans and carries on like the next thing you know Daddy will come smash Little Walter with his tire iron. She asks, "Where's he at now?"

Popeye says, " . . . Walking off down the road."

I say, "Well . . . maybe he finally got her out of his system."

" . . . He'll be back," Chloe says.

The Fish Trap

When the wardens come to dynamite us, Papa hid in the coal mine. All the people was standing around cussing and chaffing the wardens, but none of them helped out.

Papa come up the path just kind of walking fast right by the house and the dump. I tried to follow him. "Where you going, Papa?"

"Don't talk to me," he said.

He went on through the trees up the hollow to the coal mine, not running just walking fast. Sometimes he done that when he was constipated, but he had a gun.

It was a half hour later the Warden come to the house and said, "You . . . boy . . . where's old Mann?"

I called Mama.

He said, "I am the fish and game warden, and that trap is going for all time to come."

Mama come out then, and he said the same thing to her. She never buttoned her dress right and was all sweaty and hanging out in front at him. She said, "My husband run off the other game wardens, and he will run you off too."

"I know about those other fellows," he said.

"They tried to mess with my husband, and went home sadder and wiser."

"That was in the Clemens administration."

Mama looked off between the sycamore and cottonwood trees down the path to the river where the trap was. "It's a vested right," she said, "that was handed down." They was always harassing us about the fish trap. All it is is a dam the Indians built acrost the narrow east channel of the Gasconade River with a six foot gap in the middle with a slat-sided chute box that lets all the water through but keeps the fish.

"It is a violation of the game laws of the State of Missouri that has gone unchecked for more than thirty years."

"The big stones in the dam was laid there by Indians."

"I understand your feeling, Mrs. Mann. When I first come up to this picturesque spot, I stood and gazed for ten minutes at the dam and your trap. It was like I had stumbled into a scene from a hundred years ago."

"The Missouri Indians had a village on the terrace under the bluff," Mama said. "The boy finds arrowheads and scrapers there yet."

"It seemed I was far from all civilization in the Ozark hollows and woods instead of central Missouri."

Mama said, "They fought a battle in eighteen hundred and fourteen when the Sac and Fox come and tried to drive them off from the fish trap of their ancestors. They killed eleven of the Sac and Fox and scalped and gutted them and buried the guts in the corn mounds for fertilizer. It's all in the records at the courthouse. Missouris deeded the land to Antoine Soulard."

"I was at the courthouse last week," said the Warden. "The District Attorney and I were looking at those records, purely for interest."

"In eighteen hundred and sixty-two, Soulard sold out to Simeon Barker," said Mama. "He sold to Black, and in eighteen and eighty-nine, Black sold to my husband, and we fixed up the dam with ironwood logs."

"You don't own the land."

"My husband and I own the rights."

"What rights?"

"To work the trap."

"The law don't recognize the purchase of an illegal right."

"It was handed down and paid for."

"It's against the game laws to catch fish in a trap."

"The game laws are for the rich man."

"The game laws are to protect the wild creatures, for everybody."

"This here trap was before the laws. We run it to live, not for sport like some city fellow. You are taking the bread out of the mouth of this boy and his little brothers and sisters."

"From what I heard you live pretty good off of this trap, to the tune of about three thousand dollars a year cash money. Everywhere I go I hear about the fish trap. It is talked on all the trains. They ask me why I don't tear it out, and how can I expect the farmers not to trap? The merchants in Chouteau are just fed up. They try to build a grocery business, and you sell your fish at five cents a pound year in and year out. It's un-American, and I am going to enforce the law.

Where's your husband?"

"The merchants in Chouteau?" Mama said. "I thought it." She spat pretty near the Warden's boot and pulled out her snuff can like the finest lady you ever saw and took a pinch with her little finger curled and put it up there real dainty between her lip and her gum. She wasn't scared of no game warden.

"Where is your husband?" he said.

"For all you know," Mama said, "he might be up a tree with his thirty-thirty taking a bead on the back of your head."

The Warden turned around real quick, and Mama laughed the way she done when she talked about putting poison in our food and makes the hair stand up on the back of my neck. "Boy," she said, "run find your papa and tell him there's another one of them game wardens here that wants to be run off the place."

The Warden was cursing and looking around kind of nervous, and I cut down the path and up into the hollow where the old mine was.

I went in as far as the light and called, "Papa? Papa . . . it's me."

His voice come from behind me tight and hissing like a snake. He was hid up above the entrance squatting on the ledge with his thirty-thirty across his knees. "I told you to get." He was kind of runty and yellow faced.

"Papa, you scared me."

"Get on out, before—"

"Mama said. There's another warden here says he's going to dynamite the fish trap into kingdom come. He can't do that. He can't, Papa, can he?"

"I know who's here."

I argued and begged him, trying to make him come out and be a man. You could smell the tubs of mash back in the tunnel and it made me almost sick. I told him it was our right since the Indians, how it was fought over, and about the guts of the Sac and Fox in the corn mounds, and about the Warden arguing and insulting Mama.

He groaned and cursed, perched up there rocking back and forth and cursing the law and cursing me for my lip, but the Warden insulting Mama, that done it, and he climbed down.

He went a few steps down the path and stopped, holding his thirty-thirty deer rifle like he was hunting birds with it. I tried to go on past him but he put up his hand for me to stop, and when I started to ask why he slapped me all of a sudden up the side of the head so hard that I went down and sat there seeing stars.

By the time I woke up, my brother-in-law Charley that works the night shift was running down from the house to the river in just his shirt and Papa running, and I took off after them.

When I come out of the trees all the people waiting to buy fish was down on the far bank and some up on the dam shouting at the Warden and the two fellows with him and Papa and Charley running out from the near bank onto the gravel bar cursing and yelling trying to get at the Warden but the fellows that come with him had shotguns, and the Warden's team and wagon the wheels wrapped in burlap so he could sneak up on us through the bottoms, and the Warden kneeling by the chute fooling around, then he stands up and fires his shotgun once into the air and screams, "Dynamite!" and you could see it then, the fuses sputtering like snakes of fire, and you never saw folks clear off so fast falling over each other to get up that muddy bank, and their horses and teams jumping around, and one team and wagon spooked and went running away back the graded road to Chouteau.

Only Papa and Charley didn't know what to do. Papa stopped, dropped the thirty-thirty, Charley run back and Papa after him, then Papa stopped again and run back like he was going to try and snuff them fuses only it was too late, then he went toward his gun, and stopped and cut back for the bank, all quivering and shaking, running with his knees high as if the ground was red hot, and his eyes bugged out like a horse in a barn fire.

Then it went, the whole earth shook and a giant hand like Papa knocking me down, it blew the wind out of me and a lightning flash in broad daylight the sound a half second later inside your head, and rocks, logs, boards, and mud and water rose in the air like a flower, slow, up near as high as the tall flaking sycamore trees, and there was fish hanging in the air, then it all come down thump and splattering, water, fish, gravel, and mud still splashing down after, and there was a long time with no sound at all, not even a locust or a bird, and then all them folks scrambling and scurrying for the horses and wagons to get away afraid to have our misfortune rub off or the Warden give them a summons.

The river ran strong twenty foot wide where the dam was blowed out and over parts of the gravel bar that was dry before, and the pool emptied, and a couple of worthless big old gar fish lay flopping and clicking their bony scales stranded in a mud hole near me. I saw Poppa's thirty-thirty laying where the water just went down again, and I went and got it and slipped back into the willow thicket under the bank and shook off the water and dried it on my shirt.

The Warden and his men come out and they helped him up into his wagon and sidled off in different directions, quick but like they didn't want to let on how much of a hurry they was in.

I followed along through the willows then by a trail I know. The other two wasn't with the Warden now. He went along pretty quiet, the sacking on his wheels all muddy. Sometimes I was close to him, sometimes a ways off. Then he stopped and got out and started pulling at something, a net, and he just pulled it out of the water and chopped it up with his axe. I lay there behind a tangle of old roots not fifty foot away drawing a bead on him and gnats whining around trying to crawl inside my ears and my eyes and up my nose. I would have then, but it was too close up.

Further on he done it again, and inside of a half hour he chopped up three more nets and a trotline, and there ain't nothing illegal anywhere about a trotline. I almost let him have it then. I could see the cloud of gnats around his head too.

At Haun's Mill he caught a fellow in the act of sitting in his boat doing nothing and called him over to the bank and he give him such a cursing and a chewing up and down that he said if he would let him go he would tell the names of some other fellows that was seining, and he done it, and the Warden took down his name for a witness. After that he come on a johnboat tied on the bank and a net in it, and he chopped up the net and the boat too so it broke in the middle and the parts floated away. I knew then that I would do it.

I slipped on ahead about a half mile to a place where the bottoms narrows to between two bluffs and I could do it from the downstream side, then maybe I could go down to the Katy Railroad. I found a place about sixty feet up the bluff, a ledge that run around to the side and some thick cedars. He would have to pass right below on a shelf like not twenty feet wide between the limestone clift and the water. I heard his horse, and then him, whistling.

I worked the lever part way and checked the cartridge in the chamber. I cocked back the hammer, and lined up the bead in the V on where he would come.

His bay horse was shaking its head at the cloud of gnats and deer flies, walking, but wet, with sweat in the heat, then the Warden in his trooper's hat with a badge and a revolver on his hip, and behind his seat on the new green painted wagon a pump shotgun and a axe and spade. I could have spit on him, he was passing that close below, then he was moving away, and there is something about the back of a man's head and his neck that you feel sorry for him.

I had to squirm sideways to keep the bead on his head, and I must have kicked loose a rock, and it rolled down and bounced on the roadway and into the water just behind the wagon. Well, you'd have thought a panther jumped on that horse. It reared back all wild-eyed in the traces and screamed like a man. It must have been half crazy anyhow from the deer flies. The Warden spun around, and right off he saw me, then he was beating the horse on the head with his whip handle until it settled down, and I wasn't even aiming at them when I pulled the trigger. I wasn't afraid. It was more like I come this far figuring to do it, I at least had to hear the gun go off once, like after a day out hunting when you are skunked.

The horse jerked like you shocked him with electric but didn't rear or try again to run off. He just stood still, kind of shaking. I didn't shoot nowhere near that horse either. The Warden sat there on the seat of the wagon looking up at me. I almost could have spit on him. "Did you try to kill me?" he said.

I looked back not quite in his eyes but off to one side. I didn't even work the lever to put another cartridge in. The gun was still pointing at him though. ". . . No . . . ," I said.

"What were you trying to do?"

I lied, because I knew I could not do it now unless he committed something else like chopping up that good boat. " . . . Trying to scare your horse."

"Well, it don't take much to do that," he said, "with all this heat and insects."

" . . . No, sir."

"Empty your gun." He said it in a different way, quiet.

I looked at him, the horse bent down eating grass now, the reins loose. I turned the gun over and worked the lever five times, catching the dull brass cartridges in my hand.

"One more," he said.

I worked it again, the sixth, and the brass from the shot I fired made seven.

"Now, come down here . . . . Take your time. Don't fall."

He made me give him the cartridges, and he put them in his pocket.

"You are the boy from the fish trap."

"Yes, sir."

He looked at me a while, him up on the seat of the wagon and me down beside the road. "Then your name is Mann . . . ."

I looked down at my feet.

Well, he give me a talking to like I never heard. You can imagine, even if I didn't actually mean to hit him when I fired the gun.

Then he said climb up, and he would ride me a ways, so I did, and he set the horse to plodding on, and we talked a while. He said he was filing complaints at Chouteau about Papa and the seiners, and they would pay fines, but nobody was going to prison, yet, and the main thing was for this illegal fish taking and market hunting to stop before all the wildlife was killed off, because when that happened it would not be long before mankind died off too, starving in the barren land and choking on its own filth in the septic rivers. I could not follow all that, but I acted like I did.

I told him about the Indians and the big fish we took in the trap, one that its tail dragged the ground when the man that bought it tied it by the gills to his saddle horn, and many times fish that their tails hung out over the gate of a flat bed wagon.

He said that was truly remarkable, but it was finished for all time to come.

Then he said come visit at the hatchery some time, and in the spring they maybe could use a stout boy. He let me off at the Katy Railroad bridge where our river run into the Missouri. The last thing he said was he supposed I knew that for what I done I could be sent to the Booneville reformatory, and worse than that for what I was thinking about doing.

"I know," I said. I was down in the road. He let me take Papa's gun.

He reached in his pocket and handed down the cartridges. "If you tell your old man," he said, "will you get a whipping?"

" . . . Not from him."

"From your Mama?"

I didn't know what to say.

"Will you?"

"Not for what you think."

"How's that?"

"For missing."

His eyes blazed up and his lips pressed and went white but not at me exactly.

"Will you damned people ever learn?" he said. "You live like the Indians."

He shook the reins of his tired horse and went rolling along the gravel road by the tracks to Westphalia. "Well, what does that make you?" I said.

I never told Papa, or her, anything, and I just took the whipping for going off a long time without saying I would miss dinner. That was the last time though. I have not took a whipping since, and I am not about to. I did not have to kill that warden to know I could if I wanted to, and I may yet. Nights, Papa and me and Charley been working a little at a time repairing the trap.

The stones the Indians laid was mostly still there, and we hauled in more stone and ironwood logs and built the dam to just above the high water line, and the six foot gap in the center, then the beams and slats for the bottom of the trap itself to let all the water through and hold the eating size fish, and boards along the sides like a cattle chute. Papa says this place was meant by nature to be a fish trap.

Of Human Sacrifice

When I was a playwriting student at Yale Drama School, I used to grumble to my friends about our famous teacher. What warmed the cockles of his heart and made him say you had a future in the Theater, for all his erudition, was soap opera with a New York accent. But I was from Missouri, and going to make something of it.

I began to spend a good deal of time in the stacks in the neo-Gothic tower of Sterling Library reading extensively for the first time about my native state, the muddy river, and the extinct Indian tribe it is named for. In a carrel on the seventh level where almost no one else came except the stout feeble-minded women who malingered there when they were supposed to be dusting books, I found heroes. I heard voices. I saw the first Europeans toiling against the strong brown current.

I favored the accounts of returned travelers, of those who had seen unknown lands and strange tribes and reported on them to the people back home.

In his journal of the Lewis and Clark expedition, the entry for August 13, 1804, Sergeant Ordway wrote, "Set out at daylight with a breeze from the southeast, and passed several sandbars. Between ten and eleven miles, we came to a spot on the south where a Mr. McAye had a trading establishment in the year 1795 and 1796 which he called Fort San Carlos." Lewis and Clark had with them a map and table of distances on the Missouri River drawn by this man. They also carried extracts copied from the report of his voyage about the various Savage tribes they would meet. The Osage. The Kansa. The Maha. The Ponca. The treacherous Rees or Ikara. The agricultural and sedentary Mandans, and the nations beyond them to the Shining Mountains.

This Mr. McAye was my maternal grandmother's great-grandfather.

Trained as a surveyor, he had worked as a clerk and then as an Indian trader in the Canadian wilderness and what are now Minnesota, Wisconsin, and Upper Michigan for Todd & McGillivray of Montreal. When the Americans asserted their sovereignty over the old Northwest Territory, he came down to the village of St. Louis and like his patron Andrew Todd became a Spanish subject. Todd financed his great expedition, which consisted of 42 men in five pirogues and berchas and was larger than that of Lewis and Clark. McAye's reward was eleven square miles of land in Spanish grants that after the Louisiana Purchase were disallowed in the American courts.

What follows is an extract from his report to Governor de Lemos, which he wrote in French and translated into Spanish. He also spoke Gaelic and several Indian languages, and carried with him in his pirogue a case of viols. He was said to know a hundred fiddle tunes and to have taught the strathspey and jig to the Grand Detour Sioux.

THE OBJECT OF THIS VOYAGE WAS TO OPEN A COMMERCE WITH those distant nations on the upper Misuri and to discover all the unknown parts of his Catholic Majesty's dominions as far as the Pacific Ocean.

At the Mandan villages about six hundred leagues above the entrance of the river, Mr. Evans came to me with a report that the ancient Misuris were preparing a human sacrifice.

He persuaded me that we must go to them at once and solicit the release of the victim, a young Choctaw woman they had captured on the express orders of the high priest.

These Misuris are the remnant of a numerous and powerful nation which split several generations past. The larger part moved down to the mouth of the river which bears their name, then retreated after contact with white men to the Gasconade, only to be carried away in the space of a few years from the ravages of warfare and disease. The Misuris who remained unspoiled on the ancestral hunting ground are the most ancient of all the tribes on these rivers. Some have said they are descended from the vanished Mound People, who also practiced sacrifice and the eating of human flesh.

They received us with seeming affability, preparing a feast for me and my men of beans and squash and fat dog meat and offering us bedfellows from among their women. I saw some guns and ball in their possession, which they said they had traded with other nations who had traded them from white people. We then dined by special invitation five times afterward with lesser clan chiefs who it behooved us not to offend.

When we were alone in the lodge which they had vacated and provided for us and having a last dram before retiring, Bonhomme the patron of the river men began to speak. "You know I saw this thing they are doing." He witnessed it when he was living with a woman of the Grand Village Mandans and unwittingly accompanied her and some of her kinsmen on a visit to the Misuris.

He described to us how they bring the victim out and stand her between two poles resembling May poles surmounted with black flags. They extend her hands and feet and tie them to the poles. They kindle a small fire nearby from which in the old time they drew burning faggots that they apply to her breasts and groin but in modern times they heat irons for this purpose. The torture continues until she begins to sink under it.

The spy of a mock war party approaches with the same light-footed caution he would observe in mortal combat. He reports to the chief that he has discovered the enemy, that she is in an exposed position, and off her guard. The chief decides to make an immediate attack, and the warriors rush forward and impale the victim with a shower of arrows. They increase the fire until the fat exudes freely from her.

At this stage of the ceremony the women of the nation—who are corn planters—press around and oil their hoes and holding them up implore abundant harvest. Then the braves press forward and rub their arrows in the juices of the enemy to fit them for the perils of the great buffalo hunt.

We were all affected by this account, Evans to an alarming degree. A young man of extreme altruism, he came out to the New World as the agent of a Society possessed with a fancy of discovering the legendary Welsh Indians. These were supposed to be descended of the Eleventh Century wanderer Morgan y groehdd, of a fair complexion and speaking a Celtic tongue. Despite a sectarian bigotry, he had nevertheless read all Charlevoix. He would speak with a strange perturbation of mind of the martyrdom of the Jesuit missionaries Father Jogues and Father Peyoux, as they were exquisitely tortured to death by the proud Mohawk canton of the Iroquois. The son of a Methodist exhorter, he cherished a longing to break the savage heart to Christ.

Yet I must allow his good cheer and literate conversation were a solace in the desert places. Generous to a fault, once in heaving to free the piroque from a bar he burst a blood vessel and vomited a great profusion of blood, and after another day of severe exertion voided blood copiously in his urine.

ABOUT ONE O'CLOCK AT NIGHT I was awakened by some drunken revelers emerging from a nearby lodge. By the coals of the fire I could dimly see the outlines of my sleeping men. Evans was gone.

At once I looked to the priming of my brace of pistols and set them in reach under a fold of my buffalo robe. I was pulling on my boots when an Indian came through the entry tunnel into the lodge. As he beckoned I stuck the pistols into my belt and approached him.

A man of some fifty years with a freshly shaven head and an air of dignity, I had not seen him in the round of entertainments by the principal chiefs. He wore a soiled and mended black robe or soutane of the banished Jesuit order and on a scarlet ribbon an English Indian medal of the third class.

We moved to a part of the lodge well away from the fire. I was not a little astonished when he addressed me in tolerably good French. He said he came as a friend of the whites.

He told me that as a boy he was apprenticed to a shaman to learn the hunting magic and healing arts, but it was the time when the animals led by the beaver conspired to drive men from the land by the terrible diseases. Whole villages sickened and died in a few days from the running sores and putrefaction of the flesh, from the terrible thirst and voiding of the bowels until the veins burst and the sufferers passed their own intestines.

The animals withdrew from the land and would no longer give themselves up to the hunter. The reading of the shoulder blade in the hot coals no longer foretold where to stalk them. The healing arts were of no avail.

The people ceased to believe in the shamans, and the children mocked them.

So he had traveled to the Jesuits at Michilimackinac to apprentice himself to them and learn the hunting magic and healing arts of the white men.

But the diseases broke out again, and again among the people, and the arts of the white men were of no avail either, except that only a very few of the whites were afflicted because they had suffered these diseases since the beginning of time. He decided then it was not the conspiracy of the animals but the coming of the whites that brought the sickening unto death.

When the French were defeated in the wars of the white man and the Black Robes were driven from the land, he went to the English traders on the Red River of the North, and he attempted to learn the healing arts and the Book of Prayers of the English. This also was of no avail.

Then he returned to his own people, and after long fasting and sweat baths and smoking of the strong leaf, the Master of Life spoke to him in a dream and commanded him to bring his people back to the religion of their ancestors, and he revived the practice of the sacrifice and taught them to shun the whites.

For many winters the ancient Misuris prospered. The bison and elk and brewlaw returned to their lands and increased, and their fields that the women planted were fruitful of the squash and beans and maize. They were spared when the diseases struck again from time to time among other nations, and they were victorious in warfare over their enemies.

But his people had begun to covet the merchandise of the traders, and obtain it at great cost from the other nations that allowed the whites among them. They were slaying the beaver in great numbers without respect. The previous winter was long and bitter and the hunting lean. Their enemies the Sioux with guns from the white men had won victories over their war parties, and the white man's diseases had struck their neighbors the Mandans.

It was time once again to restore the faith of his people in themselves, and in the rightness of their own ways against the ways of the whites—by which indeed the white men flourished—but were the sickness unto death for the red man. It was a time that demanded they resort once again to their most powerful magic.

It was time for the sacrifice.

"I know you, Santiago MacKay," he said, revealing a command of the English tongue as well as the French. The grammar was imperfect, but his store of words never failed his native eloquence. Although I cannot pretend to record his speech exactly, he said in effect, "I know from when you are the trader for the English at Kildonan Post on the Red River of the North, and I know of the woman of the Assiniboine you take to wife there and leaved with many childrens.

"You turn your back on the English. The cause is not for me to know.

"You go to the town of St. Louis. You tell the Spanish chief that dwells there near the mouth of the River Misuri that you know the secret of the pass through the Montanas Relucientes to the South Sea. You come for the present of many golden dollars that the Great Spanish Father will give to the first white man who shows him this way.

"I declare and prophesy unto you, Santiago MacKay: Stay on the path of your journey. Let the Ancient Misuri in peace obey the religion of their ancestors as it is necessary for them to do, or you will never see again the Shining Mountains, or find the pass to the South Sea."

I knew then that this must be the dread Shaman and Prophet himself of the Ancient Misuris, the Oiseau Noir, and I could not but respect the intelligence of his savage mind. In this time of stress and religious fervor his influence among the people might well be the equal if not stronger than that of the council of temporal chiefs.

I offered him a trifling present of a brass compass, which he accepted, and a gill of brandy, which he refused.

After he had left me I sat up by the fire for some time smoking and ruminating on these things.

NEXT DAY when the chiefs and braves of the nation met me in council, I learned that fuel was already gathered and the eunuchs building the scaffold. I ommitted no argument or persuasion, however, in attempting to obtain the release of the woman. I spoke to them in words I had taken some pains to compose beforehand in my mind.

"I come to you because I was informed by one of your white brothers that you have now as a captive this Choctaw woman whom you intend to burn to the Great Star. I come to remind you of the promise you once made to Auguste Chouteau in the presence of Bonhomme the patron of the river men who sits now at my left hand. It was this: that you never would be guilty of burning another poor defenseless prisoner. Your great friend the Knife Chief and his son a few days after this promise liberated a squaw that you had fattening in your medicine lodge for that cruel purpose and sent her home to her people. This deed alone immortalized them both not only among the red men but whites also.

"You have ever since been a fortunate people. You have been blessed with good health, abundance of corn, and buffalo, and you have been successful too over your common enemies the Sioux, for it is not many moons since your village was decorated with their scalps.

"You know it was the last wish of those three great men, Auguste Chouteau, the Knife Chief, and his son that the ancient Misuris should ever think themselves too brave and too much like men to again be guilty of such a squawlike deed as that of burning a prisoner. These three wise and warm friends to the Misuris are no more.

"Their spirits are this moment looking down upon you to see you act as they requested you. The instant you depart from the promise you made to them they will blast your corn, drive off your buffalo, give your enemies power over you and leave you to be scalped and to starve. Remember, furthermore, that I tell you you will make your great father, His Catholic Majesty the Prince of Spain, angry with you as well as all your white friends and brothers.

"I therefore advise, request, and demand that you hand over to me in this place the Choctaw squaw, so that I may send her back to her friends and relations. If you do so you shall be treated accordingly. You have known whites for many winters, and we have never given you bad advice."

When nearly seven hours had been consumed in council, I was pleased and surprised to observe that the older men of the tribe seemed disposed to release the captive.

She was brought in and seated to the right of the principal chief, Antoine. Her jet black hair was gathered in a fashion different from the Misuri Women, her face a pale brown not unknown among the savages. She was a little under the average size, wearing a plain robe of buffalo and a dress cut and stitched from a Bay Company blanket. Although unkempt in her despair, she was yet in the bloom of young womanhood.

Her demeanor was modest, sitting with bowed head; then bold, as she caught and held the gaze of Evans. Then her amber eyes fixed on me.

I distributed the merchandise I had brought for the purpose of sealing the bargain, steel, flints, powder, a ration of brandy, blue beads, and the vials of hot sauce from Maxent of New Orleans that they clamor to obtain.

We were smoking a pipe over it, when my attention was arrested by a strange sound that I then perceived as the savage music of bull-roarers, gourd rattles, drums, and a haunting instrument with one string that changed pitch according to where it was stopped. The sound increased and burst upon us as those who were making it, the eunuchs of the high priest, came strutting and mincing into the lodge, followed by the Black Bird himself.

This man—or, according to the credulous, he is both man and woman—holds the priesthood by right of the sacred medicine bag handed down in his family. Chouteau claims that along with the usual herbal physics and simples, it contains hieroglyphic banner stones from the priests of the Mound People, the same who built the vanished metropolis upwards of sixty thousand souls where this river disgorges into the Mississippi in what has come to be called the American bottoms opposite the village of Saint Louis.

The claimant to the title of the Black Bird has a special power to strike terror in the hearts of his people. They believe that merely by willing it he can cause anyone who has displeased him to be afflicted with stomach cramps, to foam at the mouth, fall down in convulsions, and die a horrible death. I later found this to be true. A demented trader at Michilimackinac had given him a supply of the arsenic of lead.

He wore a mask with the recurved beak and staring eyes of a bird of prey, a mantle of black feathers from what we know as the turkey vulture, and also a kind of waistcoat and leggings of black feathers, and bird's feet. From his ears hung rings of beaten copper with a pair of segmented rattles from that breed of serpent peculiar to this country. Likewise on his ankles and wrists were circlets of these rattles, so that his every movement was accompanied by their dry buzzing sound, like a swarm of venomous insects.

The eunuchs, who elect their status by demonstrated cowardice or by refusing to participate in warfare, sang a falsetto chant punctuated with staccato barks and cries, forming a half-circle across the entry and behind the Black Bird.

The effect on the assembly of two hundred warriors in all their supposed stoicism was like electrical fluid on the leg of a frog. They visibly shrank and shuddered, some raising a hand or arm and fold of blanket to ward off the rays of malevolence.

The woman huddled together as if she expected her death blow momentarily, and went into a trance of shock.

The Black Bird removed his mask. He was indeed the same man with a freshly shaven head, prominent aquiline nose, and scowling eyes who had visited me in the night. He sat himself down facing Chief Antoine, reached for the long-stemmed pipe that rested on his knee, offered it to the Sky, the Earth, to the health of the Living, to the memory of the Dead, then took some conciliatory puffs. Antoine drew his robe around him in closer folds and appeared ill-at-ease.

The Black Bird told the council that he believed the Master of Life would be very angry if they witheld the promised sacrifice. But now that his people were making themselves the children of the whites, perhaps even without the burnt offering they would have plenty of buffalo, abundance of corn, safety from their enemies, and be spared the white man's diseases that he brings from the filth of his cities.

He was pleased at the wealth of merchandise the red children took in payment for giving up the religion of their ancestors.

No doubt the whites had more intercourse and were better acquainted than naked red men with the Master of All Things.

They should listen to us. They should please us, for they could not choose better men to take the place of the Mhatchi Manitou who causes the sun to rise and set and the seasons to follow one on another and the hunting wind to blow, who flung the stars into the sky and makes the earth fruitful with his jism.

By releasing the victim they so pleased the whites that we gave them our Jesus and promised they would live forever.

He abruptly rose, put on his beaked mask, and strode out, followed by the eunuchs beating a dirge.

Antoine stood up. "The dog lies," he said. "The whites have not told us we can live forever. We must die. They must die. The Master of Life permits neither white nor red man to live always."

He reminded them again of the promise to Chouteau and that he himself had visited the great village of the white men at the place called Saint Louis, or Pain Court, where the long trails and the waters meet. He had taken his father the Viceroy by the hand and pledged himself to oppose the barbarous rites. In language as bold as it was eloquent he urged them to release the captive, and no further opposition was heard.

In the council lodge he spoke to those already disposed to his views.

Outside were the women clamoring for the sacrifice, and also the children, and the hot-headed younger men who took the presumption of the whites to interfere in their religion as a national affront.

Antoine gave over the woman into our custody and advised us to depart with all deliberate haste.

We were moving toward the river but had not cleared the earthen dome lodges when an Indian waiting in the covered entrance of one of them sprang forward with a strung bow and arrows in hand. The red man who led our way without hesitation closed with him and wrestled the weapon from his grasp.

In a moment this fellow was succeeded by another from the same concealment, who let fly an arrow that passed through the robe and under the dress of the woman and penetrated so far into her as to inflict a mortal wound.

While she was slowly sinking to the ground, Evans stepped forward to grapple with the murderer, and a general melee ensued. As I was endeavoring to drag him off, he drew a pistol and put a ball through the head of the man.

A howl of outrage went up from the mob, and he was at once struck with arrows, and the discharge of an Indian musket.

Blood spouted from Evans' mouth and nostrils with every breath, yet he was endeavoring to speak. As I knelt close, he went into a convulsion, and lay still.

Only the immediate and forceful intervention of the partisans of Antoine prevented a general massacre of the whites. He and the other principal chiefs formed a cordon around us and our small party. He asked if his father the Viceroy at Pain Court and his Catholic Majesty the Prince of Spain would punish the ancient Misuris for killing the white man.

I made an effort to collect my wits to address him. "You greatly feared our wrath and yet have risked it. What is horrible to us nevertheless is religion to you. The point comes when we must let live.

"The death of my friend is another matter. If my heart did not burn to avenge the death of a friend, I would be less than a man.

"Yet what do I see? One white man and one red man, side by side on the yellow earth in their gore. The relations and friends of the red man have avenged his death on the white man, but they have not mutilated his body. They did not intend it as an affront to the nation of white men.

"The score is even.

"This I will say in my report to my father, who is also your father, his Catholic Majesty the Prince of Spain."

After a short consultation among the chiefs present, and although the insurrection of the xenophobic party of the Black Bird yet raged and the tranquility of the village was far from restored, we were told to depart in peace.

As we moved slowly toward the river bank with the remains of Evans wrapped in a Bay Company blanket, we saw the body of the woman dragged to the head of a ravine that was only a few rods out of our path. To this point came a long line of warriors followed by the swarm of women and children. First the men passed, each smearing a war club or some other weapon in the blood of the victim. By the time we had reached the river, it was the turn of the women with their flint hoes and picks, and the naked children.

WE WINTERED among the Mandans.

In the spring when we came again to the village of the Ancient Misuris, no smoke issued from the smoke holes and the fat dogs skulked away without raising a clamor. A cloud of ravens and turkey vultures rose from the earthen domes, filling the air with their thin cries and obscuring the sun.

I entered the nearest lodge. It was a charnel house. My gorge rose at the stench from the putrifying flesh of scores of bodies lying side by side on the packed earth.

The scene in each lodge that I visited was the same.

In one there stood a wooden cage that must have held the Choctaw woman fattening for the sacrifice. On a dais covered with buffalo robes in his ceremonial garb of black feathers lay the Black Bird, a Charleville musket cradled in his arms. The ball had entered under the point of his chin and burst the roof of his skull.

The Ancient Misuris were extinct.

WHEN I ATTEMPTED to ascend further, I was prevented by the Yancton Sioux.

As we launched the piroque into the dull brown waters the boatmen—in heedless jollity at the prospect of return to civilized life—took up one of their songs to the tune of Bonhomme's fiddle.

> Bonsoir, le maitre et la maitresse
> Et tout le monde du logis
> Pour le dernier jour de l'anee . . .

A Judge's Tale

The Sheriff Mr. Smith and the Circuit Attorney Mr. Bryant both came to my room before I had time to change my clothes. They told me that three days ago a man named Cletus, the property of Mr. Meriwether, committed an assault with a pruning knife upon a Mr. Durrett from which he very nearly died and had lost the use of his right arm. On the following day a man named Jim, belonging to Mrs. Howard, was charged with an attempted rape upon a white woman named Mary Habscot at a farm on Thrailkill Branch. Both of these servants were in jail.

On the same day a man called Tyree, belonging to Dr. Price at Arrow Rock, had seized a white girl some ten years of age out picking blackberries and dragged her off into a thicket and committed an unspeakable act upon her. That night he was summarily examined and hanged and his corpse left on display for the instruction of the negroes.

I had come to try a man named John, belonging to Giles Kiser, for the brutal murder of young Mr. Benjamin Hinton in his wood yard at Malta Bend. I asked if there was danger of popular violence, and both Mr. Smith and Mr. Bryant said they thought there was.

"Then we must have a posse," I said.

The Sheriff Mr. Jacob Smith replied, "I do not believe we can get an effective posse."

I was more than a little surprised.

"Not in Saline County at the present time."

I asked, "Can you guarantee the prisoners at least for the sitting of the court?"

Smith looked to Mr. Bryant for assent and said he believed that he could.

Scarcely a week after burying my dear young wife and our babe that died in her travail, I had spent the night at Grand Pass and arisen at three in the morning to coax my broken-down horse over the bad roads and hoped to have time to rest and compose myself. Instead I went down to the public room and made inquiries of the host and others gathered there for breakfast as to the state of feeling of the people.

They told me it ran high. I might soon expect three distinct exasperated parties in and about the court house—relatives and friends of the outraged woman Mary Habscot, of Mr. Durrett who was cut, and of the murdered young man. His friends soon after the crime on the 13th of May last had converged on the town in several wagons and well armed so that Sheriff Smith was obliged to transfer the prisoner in haste to the jail of an adjoining county.

"We are tired of you running them off," said a coarse fellow with a tumbler of whiskey beside his plate of bacon and grits.

Another man said, "The owner of the scoundrel who cut on Will Durrett mounted him on a fast horse, started for the nearest railroad station, and was about getting him on the cars."

"What are the darkies to think?"

Since Missouri has no law to compensate the owner when a slave is hanged, this is a general complaint.

I felt the full force of my responsibility. If I ordered a posse and as the Sheriff feared it was not effective, I would be at the mercy of popular violence. Not in the least expecting any attempt to seize the prisoners until toward evening, I resolved to trust to what moral force the court could exert for the time being.

I took my place upon the bench at half past eight in the morning and empanelled a grand jury and spoke to them in the usual way. Then in a mild yet firm manner I addressed the people who had crowded in to fill the court room. I said, "I hope there is no foundation for the rumors of popular violence I have heard . . . . However you may justify yourselves to each other if you were to take the prisoners from the officers of the law—especially now that court is in session to try this case—it would not be so easy to justify yourselves to the world. I believe I need only hint at this for it to be distinctly understood: The enemies of our institution would rejoice in such a scene!

"If they are guilty the prisoners in a short time will receive in a legal manner the punishment due their crimes. I know that your feelings are irritated and exasperated—and justly so, but if you act now in a summary manner . . . it could not be excused as it might have been in the heat of the moment . . . when the offenses were just committed and no court convened for their trial . . . . I exhort the older and thinking men among you to let your influence prevail."

As I made these remarks I glanced rapidly round the court room and thought I could see assent on the countenances of many and looks of defiance on but few.

The Grand Jury then retired but soon returned with indictments against John for the murder of Benjamin Hinton, Jim for the attempted rape of Mary Habscot, and Cletus for assault with intent to kill William Durrett. I assembled a petit jury to try John, who was then brought in, and I appointed two young men recently from Kentucky, Ralph P. Strother and Joseph L. Hutchinson, to represent him. On such short notice I knew they could mount no credible defense but given the tension in the courtroom and ugly mood, a petition for delay was unthinkable. Young Strothers and Hutchinson held a brief conference with John, and he entered a plea of not guilty.

After his opening remarks the prosecutor Mr. Bryant called as witnesses Mr. Martin A. Gauldin, the slaves Harvey and Banjo, and the jailer W.W. Arnett.

Benjamin Hinton, 33 years of age and the son of a prominent Lafayette County farmer, with his slave Banjo and his partner Giles Kiser and Kiser's slave John chopped and sold wood to the steamboats from the yard of Hinton's cabin in the Teteseau bottoms on the Missouri River.

On Saturday morning May 14 his man Banjo went to his crib to rouse him and build his fire. He found him with his head split open weltering in his own blood and a bloody ax beside him on the floor. His steamer trunk had been forced open and the money he kept there was gone.

Gauldin testified that he had been told John proposed to two other servants that they kill Hinton for his money and run away to Kansas, that John deposited ten bloody dollars with his man George, and on the morning after the crime his shirt was spattered with blood. John was arrested with a blood-soaked ten-dollar bill in his possession and a search of his wife's cabin on Gauldin's place revealed an additional thirty-eight dollars hidden in a mitten belonging to Hinton. Gauldin earlier had testified to this effect before Magistrate H.D. Doak, causing John to be confined in Marshall in the Saline County jail.

While there on the report of Mr. Arnett John confessed his crime. He bore a grudge against Hinton for threatening to chastise him, saying only his master Mr. Giles had a right to do that. He took Giles' horse and stole away in the night and rode the six miles to Hinton's cabin by the river. He knocked on the door saying his master sent him. Hinton came and answered the door in his nightshirt saying, "Is that you, John?" When he turned to light a candle John struck him down with a faggot of wood. He then finished the work with Hinton's own ax.

John was said to have confessed in the mistaken belief that he would be released to the custody of his master, who would then sell him down south so that he might escape serving time in the penitentiary. The result was rather that on hearing of John's confession Hinton's friends and neighbors in Saline and in Lafayette County decided—they were reported to have said, "Judge Lynch will hold a special term and try the murderer with fire!"

Accordingly before dawn on Friday the 27th of May nine wagon loads of armed men together with others on horseback gathered north of Marshall at the bridge over the Salt Fork and at first light came clattering into town and went to the jail and demanded that John be handed over to them. To their chagrin Sheriff Jacob Smith had on the previous day transported John to the jail in Boonville forty miles away.

At a meeting in the courthouse also attended by a number of townspeople they narrowly decided against riding on to Boonville to deal with John there and instead to petition for a special session at the earliest convenience of the court. My hearing the case on the 19th of July rather than at the next regular term for Saline in November was in response to this petition. I note these facts not as material to the servant's guilt or innocence but in the light of what followed.

The trial of John lasted some two and a half hours at the end of which the jury rendered a verdict of guilty of murder in the first degree.

As is customary in such cases—but also considering how they had not been appointed until the day of the trial and their youth and inexperience—I remarked to the prisoner's attorneys that I would give them time to prepare motions in arrest of judgment or for a new trial if they so desired. At this point I saw impatience on the countenances of many in the crowd for me to pronounce the expected sentence. The thought flashed across my mind that if in their hearing I ordered the prisoner back to the jail, he would never reach there.

I proceeded to have the servant Jim brought before me to be tried for the attempted rape of Mrs. Habscot. The rush to the bar was such that the Sheriff could scarcely keep it clear. I empanelled a jury and administered to them the oath.

When dinner hour arrived I made no formal adjournment but rather declared a recess of one hour and ordered the prisoners John and Jim to remain in the court house in the charge of the Sheriff. I turned aside however and nodded for Smith to come to the side of the bench and privately told him as soon as the crowd dispersed—as I supposed it would—to convey John back to the jail.

I remained upon the bench observing the movements of the people. Many did leave. But the court room was not cleared as is usual on such occasions, and I saw men advancing into the bar whose countenances I thought plainly indicated their purpose.

I came down from the bench and stood by the prisoner and inquired for the Sheriff who at that time I could not see. One of the deputies told me he was not far off. I remarked, "The prisoners are in no danger so long as I am with them . . . Will you please go and tell Mr. Smith to come to me."

He came. I said to him, "Take John to jail and I will go with you."

Smith started with the servant, I close behind. Before we reached the gate of the court house yard I observed to my right hand crowds getting over the fence and others coming down the street in the direction of the jail. Their purpose will be readily guessed. Smith quickened his pace and to such a degree that my unwieldy body with a crippled leg could no longer keep up.

The prisoner reached the jail and was locked in by Mr. Arnett.

When I approached a large crowd had assembled in front of the jail door, and a man by the name of Shackleford stood on the steps delivering a harangue to incite them to acts of violence.

I took aside the Circuit Attorney Mr. Bryant and urged him to address the crowd and see if he could not appease them. He attempted to press his way through to the mounting block at the curb but shortly returned and said that Mr. Shackleford was as respectable as any man in the county—the justice of the peace for Grand Pass township—and if such as he had taken the matter in hand, it was all over with the prisoners.

"Are you armed?" I asked him.

"Sir?" he said in some surprise.

"Do you have a pistol about your person?"

"No, sir," he replied.

I hold it beneath the dignity of the bench to go armed, but at that moment I longed to have a Colt revolver or the ten-gauge shotgun that brought down many a high-flying goose in my youth with a charge of double aught buck that I might press the muzzle of it to the head of this fellow Shackleford and defy them to lay hands on the prisoner.

I had no such recourse and could only stand mute as the silver-tongued scoundrel practiced his sophistry on the credulous mob.

"Yet our Sheriff felt he must run off the negro to the next county

. . . !" he cried. "And what was the natural consequence on the minds of the servants? The scenes which followed too plainly tell. Will Durrett in his own yard . . . orders this man Cletus . . . who has been repeatedly warned . . . to keep away from his house. What is the consequence? The negro slashes him with a pruning knife and very nearly kills him . . . and would have . . . but for the courageous interference of Durrett's wife.

"And what followed this outrage? Cadet Meriwether, the owner of this vicious negro, immediately mounts him on a fast horse, starts for the railroad station, and would have gotten him clean away . . . . The only punishment for his crime under our law is thirty-nine lashes, a crime for which a white man would receive twenty years in the state penitentiary."

At this the crowd stirred with assent and here and there a fervent, "Amen."

"The practice of running off negroes and selling them out of reach of the law . . . persuades them they can commit almost any crime . . . and because they are so valuable to their owners . . . go scot free.

"And what is the consequence?

"In rapid succession . . . we find two more offenses in our neighborhood . . . more heinous than either of the first! A delicate woman in her house—attending to her daily business while her husband is at work in the fields and out of reach of her cries for help—is brutally assailed and most shamefully abused. An insolent negro tears at her clothing, throws her down on the floor, and attempts to rape her.

"In the other a girl ten years old is out with her little brother gathering blackberries and not apprehending the slightest danger . . . when a depraved negro named Tyree . . . the property of Dr. Price . . . naked in order to disguise himself . . . rushes upon her . . . rudely drags her into a thicket . . . a child of ten . . . and with savage brutality . . . commits a crime of lust upon her in a manner I shudder to contemplate.

"Take these acts together.

"I must speak plainly. I wish to be understood. If one of the fair daughters of our land is violated or attempted to be violated by a negro, I will use all the energies of my nature and all the powers that God has given me to bring him to a speedy and terrible punishment.

"Others may call it mob law. Well, it was mob law when Andrew Jackson drove the Legislature of Louisiana from their halls and closed the doors. It was mob law when he bombarded Pensacola and hung Arbuthnot and Ambrister . . . . It was mob law when the laboring men of Boston disguised themselves as Indians . . . and threw the tea overboard! It was mob law when the people of France hurled the Bourbons from the throne and crushed out the dominion of the priests . . . and established a new order of things! They did not quail at shedding blood . . . and they saved France!

"Abolitionists and agitators come among us. They seduce our servants with tales of running off to Kansas and create a spirit of insubordination and insolence among them. Kiser's John split young Benjamin Hinton's head with an axe to steal forty dollars and flee with his doxy to Kansas. The signs of the times are writ large across the sky! I know of no reason . . . when the powers that be fail to protect us . . . why we should not have a little mob law in the State of Missouri and County of Saline!"

At this the crowd was unleashed in a sudden rush upon the jail house door. Arnett the jailer refused to give up the key. He made for a single man what defense he could but was overpowered, the key taken from him. The prisoners John and Cletus—the latter having never been before the court—were taken from the jail to a grove near the town some two hundred yards more or less from the public square.

In the meantime a party appeared in the courthouse where Jim—whom a jury had been impanelled to try—was in custody and forcibly wrested him from the two deputies, as one of them told me presenting a pistol and threatening to shoot if they resisted.

Jim was taken to the same grove as Cletus and John.

Cletus was about thirty years of age and had the reputation of being a vicious negro. Certainly he had the worst countenance of the three. He was worth about $1000, his owner a grand nephew of the famed explorer. His offense was not so great as John's it is thought solely because the man whose life he came very near taking was saved by the heroism of his wife. A rope was adjusted about his neck and he was swung up to the limb of a walnut tree. He did not struggle and died apparently easy.

Jim was 32 to 35 years of age and worth probably $1000, his owner a widow of some property who had hired a clever young attorney to cast doubt on whether he—known as Big Jim—or another man known as Little Jim was the one who had committed the assault. He struggled hard to free himself of those who had him in charge. To the mob his offense was the blackest of the three yet the law does not recognize it as equal to either of the others in that the punishment is not so severe.

Their intention at first was to burn Jim but he finally was swung up on the same limb with Cletus where he struggled for some time, dying hard.

John was about twenty-three years of age and a valuable slave worth perhaps $1,500. He had an open and intelligent countenance and spoke very freely with all those willing to hear him as he was chained to the trunk of the tree. He had confessed his guilt shortly after his first examination, but not until Tuesday did he state that he had an accomplice. We have no means of knowing whether it was the fear of death or the hope of punishing his enemies that brought this last confession, which is not generally credited. A white man, John averred, was his accomplice and shared the gains.

He was heard through.

Then Shackleford himself—the duly sworn justice of the peace of Grand Pass township—applied the match beneath the combustibles piled around him. When the flames began to hiss about him, and the fire to penetrate his flesh, John first seemed to realize that he was to expiate his crime in that dreadful manner, for all along he seemed to have fed upon the fond belief that an honest confession would mitigate his punishment. His tormentors muttered among themselves that they did not hear him making his peace with a more terrible Judge than Lynch, and in his dying he prayed more to those around him than to the One above. The ghastly effects of the fire could be seen in the futile attempts of the poor wretch to move his feet. As the flames gathered about his limbs and body, he commenced the most frantic shrieks and appeals for mercy, for death, for water. He seized his chains. They were hot and burned the flesh off his hands. He would drop them, and catch at them again and again. Then he would repeat his cries, but all to no purpose. He lived from six to eight minutes from the time the flames wrung the first cry of agony from his lips, the inhalation of the blazing fire suffocating him in the end. His legs and arms were burnt off, and his body but remained a charred and shapeless mass, bones and flesh alike burned into a powder.

I am so minute with all I had to do or that was done so far as I know in this matter in the expectation that news of it will appear in papers across the Union and the facts knowingly as well as unknowingly misrepresented.

Worn down as I am with fatigue and loss of sleep I feel hardly competent to form a correct judgment about anything. My feelings as a man as well as a judicial officer have been cruelly wounded, whether intentionally or not I will not now undertake to say. To find myself without the aid of the people and unable to keep the prisoners from being dragged from the halls of justice by violence and hanged and burnt in the sight of the courthouse was a blow like a thunderbolt in a cloudless sky that I hope and trust I never shall suffer again.

Already Shackleford and his ilk have sent high-toned letters to the Marshall *Democrat* to justify their acts and threaten like violence to anyone who would bear witness against them or call them to account. On the other hand those whose hearts bleed for the Negro put the onus on me for what I failed to prevent.

Even if I were able to render effective service in the 6th Judicial Circuit of Missouri after the enormities committed here, I am disinclined to attempt it. I have written to Judge Gamble that rather than remain in a venue from which only dishonor can result, I have chosen to resign from the bench. In the anarchy the denizens of Saline County have created for themselves, let them rend each other limb from limb like dogs and bears in the pit.

Strawberries

Strawberries was to get into and get out of. Mama took one look at Francine and said, "There's trouble." But try and tell me that.

She said she come from Aurora and needed money bad because she hoped to commence her studies in the fall in the Harris normal school at St. Louis. She was staying in a big old miner's tent with three other girls and the family of one of them that all come out from town picking on their vacation. For the season when the strawberries come ripe just about everybody in southwest Missouri helps to pick like it was their patriotic duty in the World War and we was going to whip Kaiser Bill by how many cars we filled. The migrants from Arkansas help out and some from Louisiana and Texas and later they move on for the wheat in Kansas.

I got talking to her the first day dinner hour. I never told her how old I was. I am tall for my age and they allow me to give out the tickets, eight cents for each tray of four boxes at the two cents a box.

We picked until seven in the evening, and then I was going to drive the truck in. She sat in the seat up next to me, two of her girlfriends beside her, one in the other's lap, and some broken down old miner from Joplin on the running board.

I let them off in the square and drove around to wait in line at the depot to unload.

Ever' night some of them rode in with me.

Then one night it was just her. She said she didn't need to go up into town, and when I pulled into the line she stayed in the cab. There was old trucks and wagons full of the fresh picked berries stretched out a quarter mile ahead of me to the railroad tracks, the shapes of the church steeple and water tower, the elevator and tall trees, and the long shed and mules and trucks all flat and black against the twilight, lightning bugs out in the grass, and people talking low to one another to pass the time. It would be a good two hours before I got to the graders and a half hour after that before our load was safe in the express car for St. Louis and checked in the book. Already they was a dozen more loads pulled up behind me.

We sat looking out past the squashed bugs on the windshield at the yellow and purple sky in the west. The top of her head come just to my eyes. She was like a little girl then, and I was holding her, only ever' few minutes I would hear folks hollering to move up the truck in the line.

Mama bawled me out for getting it in late. Then she said, "You let them town girls alone."

I was trying to get past her between the kitchen table and the cook stove. "I seen you and that Francine," she said.

I said, "Well, I'll be going to bed."

"You leave them good pickers alone, you. It's harder to find enough one year to the next. A hulking boy like you . . . the next thing I know they'll up and quit and all the berries just rot on the vine."

"I never . . ."

"Your clothes rumpled . . . lip rouge on your shirt."

"Well, I—"

"Old enough to be your mother."

"She ain't but just going to start in the normal school."

"You mind, or I'll run her off the place."

"But you just said . . ."

She had laid her head down on the red and white oil cloth table crying.

I slunk off to my bed in the hot attic. I would rather have her cuss and holler at me all week long than make her cry.

The next day I slipped extra tickets to Francine when she come in with her trays of berries. They was like ordinary moving picture show tickets on big rolls, purple, light green, yellow, and pink. At picking season you could use them like money at the stores where you was regular trade. Every Saturday the pickers turn in the tickets for cash money. It takes upwards of twenty-five thousand pickers to get in the southwest Missouri strawberry crop, all in the last week of May and first two weeks of June.

That night Francine was off with her girlfriends, but the next night she rode in with me again. She was wearing a shirtwaist and unhitched herself and put my hand inside on her skin so I was afraid to bruise her like when you get behind picking in a hot spell and the strawberries dead ripe, and the fellow behind honking his horn for me to move up or lose my place in line. On the way back she said, "Oh, this is just terrible . . . I wish there was someplace to go . . . ."

I said I had to get the truck home but I maybe knew a place.

I left her off and put the truck away and went in sure to make enough racket and Mama in the kitchen anyhow saying least I was in early. I went up, and right out again onto the little roof over the front step and jumped to the ground and run the half mile around the edge of the hollow to the pickers' camp at Mt. Gilead meeting house. In a while she come out by the hitching shed, and I taken her back by the sinks and through the oak and hickory woods to the growed-over road and path into the hollow down by the spring run. We was walking on the packed gravel and hard mud to where you can see the chimley cave, then up the clay and fallen rock to it, then back along by the bluff face to where you don't see the real cave until you are on top of it.

"Where are you taking me?" she asked.

I showed her.

"In that wet muddy old cave?"

"It's dry," I said. I got down between the two pine trees and the bluff and duck-walked down, tugging her by the hand so she had to stoop and hitch up her skirt and she come half sliding and slipping in against me onto the dry clay.

"What if something is in here?"

I said I would kill it.

"You and who else?"

"I'm bigger than Papa."

She sniffed, and then she said she had to get back, Valerie's Mama would bawl her out.

"But you said . . . ."

She already was up out of the cave.

"I'll fix it nice. I'll show you . . . ."

But she would not say a word until we was almost back to Mt. Gilead meeting ground, and then she just kissed me cool as ice on the forehead like a little brother and said, "We mustn't get carried away."

After she left me I went home to the barn and taken a bale of mulching straw and rolled it down to the woods and all along the edge of the hollow to over where the cave is at, and I thought of just letting it go the forty feet and maybe catch on the two pine trees, but it might not, or bust open, so I went back and got three old plowlines, and back over to the cave, and tied the lines together and lowered it to in front of the cave, and then I had to go up the hollow a ways to a ravine where I could climb down and then around to the cave and untie the bale and roll it down inside, break it open, and spread the straw, only it weren't thick enough so I went and got another one and let it down and spread it, and then a third bale, and when I got home the whippoorwills was closing down and the morning birds tuning up, and I was too tired to climb up to my window and went and slept an hour in the barn and come in the kitchen when Papa was cooking up breakfast and he only kind of winked and asked if I wanted two eggs or three.

The hot spell come on then, and it was a hundred degrees in the shade, and more berries come ripe in a day than we could hardly keep up with.

Saturday evening Mama was at the old card table under the burr oak tree taking their tickets and paying out money. There was the drunk old miner from Joplin, two families of migrants up from Arkansas, a mean-looking Texan with a knife cut that looked like he just escaped from jail, the two town girls Meg and Valerie, and Valerie's folks and the two little brothers from Aurora, and Francine.

When it was her turn, Mama said, "My, Francine, you surely had a good week."

I never saw her so embarrassed. That is one thing about Francine, she almost always has a come-back. Not much bothers her. But Mama did. I could see her turn all red even in the smoky lantern light. "I need the money, Mrs. Craig," she said.

"She's a worker," I said.

Mama took a long look at me, and then she paid out.

Everybody else was getting about eleven or twelve dollars. Francine took in seventeen.

Most of them worked a half day Sunday except Valerie's family going to church, and in the rows between the heavy berry vines the sweat poured down until you was just soaking inside your clothes and the sweat in my eyes, and the ticks and chiggers besides.

I taken the day's load in at supper time and only had to wait forty minutes. So I drove on to the pickers' camp and inquired for Francine.

Her and Valerie and Meg was setting around under the tent fly around a fold-up table fanning theirselves, their skirts hitched up and their shirtwaists tied on their stomachs showing off their belly buttons. "Hey, boy," said Valerie. "Take us for a ride." Francine said I couldn't, my Mama would whip me if I didn't run the truck home. They fooled around and give me some lemonade, then Francine said, "There has to be a way to cool off around here." I said the Shut-ins. "Where's that?" she asked.

"James River."

"How far?"

"The river ain't but a mile down the hollow, but the good swimming hole is three miles around by the roads."

"I'll die if I have to walk two more steps," said Valerie.

I thought a minute and said, "I maybe could drive you around, and take the truck home, and come back."

"Who says you have to come back?" said Meg, who had black

hair and a long upper lip.

"Who says I have to drive you around?" I said, and Francine says, "Well, are we going or not?"

The orange red sun was hanging over the chat piles in the west refusing to go down. The other two was in back on account of the heat and no strawberries to look out for. Just Francine rode in the cab. I reached out, but she moved my hand off her leg onto the gear shift.

I drove up to the Nixa Road and turned east down that hollow by the limestone clifts through the woods and across the river on the rickety bridge and over the bottoms in new corn to the high bluff on the other side the top golden in the last hazy light, and right around past Seligmann cemetery to the creek hollow on the other side where the road climbed up onto the prairie again only that was where I stopped.

I climbed down and went to open the door for her and showed them the way by the spring run through the woods to the Shut-ins where the river takes a sharp turn from east to south against the bluff and the water is more than fifty foot deep and a kind of blue chalky green.

Valerie and Meg run on ahead and Francine hung back with me, then she run on ahead too to the big flat mossy stones on the edge, and they all taken their shoes and sat with their legs in the water laughing and carrying on.

The James there is a hundred foot wide and acrosst on the far bank was tall sycamores and cottonwoods, and on the side we was on the high bluff and oak and hickory on top of that. "Now run take the truck home to Mama," Meg said.

I said maybe I didn't have to just yet.

Valerie said they didn't want Mama down on them.

"Maybe I was studying to take a swim too," I said.

Meg and Valerie was talking and laughing together, and I knowed it was about me.

"Say, boy," said Meg, "how come you give Francine extra tick-ets?"

"You hush!" Francine said.

"Your mamma knows," Valerie said.

"If you give us extra tickets, you can stay and swim," Meg said.

I looked at the ground.

"Pay us all three cents a box and you can do anything you want," she said.

Valerie and Francine both hollered at her to hush.

I looked at Francine.

"You better go on . . . ," she said.

I looked at her and I didn't care what the other two said but I felt so low and mad I nearly cried. " . . . I maybe could fetch you back," I said.

"That might be nice."

I drove around home, and the sun was just down but still ninety degrees, and Papa was in his barrel stave hammock between two walnut trees and Mama on the front step fanning herself and listening to the preaching on the radio.

I told him I took some friends of mine to the Shut-ins and asked could I take the truck and fetch them.

Mama said, "That boy is to drive the truck in to the depot with the berries and straight home."

Papa said it sure was early for such a hot spell.

"You know whenever he thinks he can get away with it he is out joy riding . . . . Besides he ain't licensed . . . and his friends is the town girl pickers that I already told him to leave them alone."

Papa said for me to go on.

I did not mean to sneak up on them. I left the truck and went along the path down through the woods by the spring run. I heard them laughing and splashing around and saw the bare wet back of one of them, Meg, and as I come nearer their clothes piled on the rock. I saw Valerie and Francine out in the water.

Francine come in and climbed out on the rock, her skin gleaming wet in the twilight. She stood sideways then turned and saw me, and she never said nothing. I only saw a woman all naked before once when I walked in on Mama chasing a hound that got in the house and she screamed and hollered and still will hold it up to me.

Meg turned and I saw her too all heavy in front, but when she saw me she squealed and covered herself with her hands, and she jumped in the water.

Francine jumped in the water then too. I went out on the rock, but I could not see them good down in the water. They was all together whispering and squealing and giggling and whispering some more. They was planning something.

They come all swimming up toward me, and Meg reached up her hand and said, "Hey, boy, help me out." And as I taken her hand Francine said, "Help me too," and I give her my other hand, and they both pulled at once, and I went flat out into the water in my overalls and shirt and shoes and nearly drowned.

Taking them back was the same, the other two in truck bed and Francine up beside me only she let me take her hand and she held my arm along the top and then down a little along the inside of her leg and the back of my elbow against her there where she was soft like ripe berries, and I drove in low gear the whole three miles to Mount

Gilead meeting house.

The other two got down and Francine told them she would be along in a while, her arm on the top and inside of my leg and just touching me there, and then we got out and walked down the overgrowed road into the hollow that petered out into just a path with little wild roses growing beside and the trees laced together overhead. I never even closed the doors of the truck.

We walked along the packed gravel in the last light from the west, the stars coming out, and flowers on the bottom, blue-eyed mary and violets, and she had her arm around my waist, then I helped her up to the cave. It was still hot outside but cool as soon as we was down inside.

She felt of the straw, and I told her about bringing it the half mile from our barn. She wanted to see where we was at so I lit a candle end. The cave was stoop height, about ten foot wide, and the front room went back about forty feet to a dome like with them stone icicles hanging down, and it turns right then left again getting narrow so you can just crawl. She was satisfied coming back just to the little dome room and looking up at them stalac things she called them.

We went back out onto the straw and I stuck the candle end in a niche in the wall, the flame making a ball of light maybe twelve foot across showing the gray and brown walls and flat ceiling of a different kind of darker rock and the straw and her kneeling looking at me her shirtwaist wet from the swimming.

I knelt looking at her. I said, "I love you."

"Don't be silly," she said.

I reached out, and she held my hand against her cheek and then she was unfastening her shirtwaist, and I begun to shake.

I thought that makes me a man now, only I didn't feel a whole lot different. Well, I did, except I was shaking. I leaned over and out onto my hands, and it touched her but not just right and I was shaking and she only touched to guide me and I was thinking *This is Her* and it happened all on her hand and on her there.

She give a little cry like spilt milk and I was pretty nearly wishing I never was born, when she pulled me to her saying, ". . . Don't fret," and holding me, stroking the back of my neck.

Then she reached down and after some fooling around we got me tucked up inside her. "Lay still," she said. "Put everything out of your mind." I did like she said, and after a spell I commenced to grow inside her until I had a good old hard-on again, so we done it right after all. I fucked her. Three times. Only she don't like me calling it that. "Making love," she says, then she laughs when I say I love her.

When I drove her back to the camp ground in the truck, she put her arm around me so sweet and her head against my shoulder. I never tried to go in the house but just slept in the barn.

The next day Mama wasn't even talking to me. She followed Francine around though and her two friends, harassing them, saying they didn't leave enough stems on, then they got too much leaves and trash in the boxes, then they was picking too many culls and green berries, then the stems was too long.

In that heat I never blamed Francine when she answered back, and Mama said a few more things.

When Papa come and told her to let them be, that was the last straw. "They can just clear off," she said. "They are fired."

"No, they ain't," Papa said.

Mama went walking off to the house because nobody was going to see her cry.

That day when I could, I give Meg and Valerie extra tickets too.

At dinner hour Francine was talking to Papa, and when I asked him he looked like maybe he would answer sharp but then he told me, "She asked for three cents."

Papa has partly gray partly brown hair with kind of pointy ears and he is only a half inch taller than Mama and I am taller than both of them but skinny. Girls and women look at Papa on the street, and if the fiddler don't give out he will dance all night long.

"She says in this heat and the heavy crop, they agreed they should all get three cents."

"You giving it to them?"

"I have to talk to your Mama."

That night I never saw Francine or any of them at all. When I went by the pickers' camp only Valerie's folks and some old people was there. They told me everyone went to a meeting at Boaz.

In the morning she wouldn't hardly talk to me. I told her I was thinking of leaving here the way Mama was acting, and I would go to St. Louis where the Harris normal school that she planned to attend was at and find me some kind of job and we could get married.

"Hush," she said. "Don't talk crazy." Her hands moved among the blunt star-shaped leaves, her fingers wet with the juice.

"I love you," I said.

She went on picking like she wanted me to go away.

"I'll see you tonight," I said.

"I can't."

"After I come back from the depot . . . I have to . . . "

"I'm doing something else."

"What?"

" . . . A meeting," she said. "Now go away."

"I'll come too."

"You can't."

"I will."

"It will be over."

"Then you can see me."

"I can't."

"You have to. We—"

"Here comes your Papa."

Papa come up in his yellow cowboy boots and his voice kind of laughing he,says, "Is this boy bothering you, Francine?"

"Not at all, Vernon," she says to my Papa.

I slunk off wanting to wring his neck and hers too.

The next day was the strike.

Francine and the girls and the old miner and the families from Arkansas and the jailbird Texan was lined up acrosst the field when we come out, and Francine said they wasn't going to work until the pay was three cents a box.

"Then you ain't going to work no more around here," Mama said.

"Nobody else can work here either," said Francine.

"I never heard of such a thing," said Mama.

"That's a strike," Francine said.

"We're organized," said Meg.

"This here is our place," Mama said. "And you can just clear off."

Francine and the girls sat down.

"Vernon, fetch the sheriff," Mama said.

"If you can find him," said the Texan.

"What do you mean?" Papa asked.

"This ain't the only strawberry patch having itself a strike," the Texan said.

He was telling the truth. Almost all the fields around Republic was struck, every single one around Boaz, and most of them at Clover and Nixa, Chesapeake, McKinley, Marionville, Hurley, Crane, and Verona, and half of them at Aurora.

While Papa was gone finding out, Mama went to pick what she could.

The old miner said, "Say, you can't do that."

Well, Mama had a fit. "Don't you never try to tell me what I can do at my own place!" she said. "The next thing you know some out-of-work hotel chef is going to come in my kitchen and say I have to pay him to cook my own family's dinner, and some St. Louis whore is going to come and say I have to pay her to do that for me in my own bed with my husband!"

Valerie and Meg was talking to Francine, and after a while Francine said, "It's not allowed in a strike."

Valerie said, "She can't pick enough to matter."

"It's not allowed," said Francine.

"Just try and stop me," Mama said, and she taken some baskets and went down the row picking a mile a minute.

"You, boy," Mama called without taking her eyes off what she was doing, "Get some of them baskets and help your mother."

I looked at Francine but she like to never saw me staring right through at someplace way off where the sky met the land.

"It ain't allowed," I said.

"Help your mother," said Valerie.

"You better not," said Francine.

"If you eat at my table you do like I say," said Mama, still looking just at where her hands was flying through the vines.

If Francine wasn't so hard and kind of far away, I never would of done it. Except I felt sorry for Mama all alone against everybody and the strawberries was how my own folks made out. So I taken up some baskets and went to picking but far away in the field as I could get from Mama.

The old blue school bus come out on the yellow dusty road from Republic, and Francine and them made the line across between the road and the field again. It stopped, and Papa and then the new pickers climbed down, stretching, spitting, scratching, three colored, two Indians, an old drunk Cajun with bleeding gums, and four hard-looking women. Only the new ones refused to go in the field as long as Francine and them was lined up there.

Papa talked to them a while and then Mama and then Papa again, and Mama went and drove the truck off saying she was going to the store to telephone.

Then the sheriff and a truck full of soldiers come and said they was going to arrest the strikers.

The two Arkansas families went peaceful, climbing up into the army truck, but the old miner and the Texan and Francine and them put up a fight. The soldiers was just boys and didn't know how to do and some of them got all scared and yelling and hollering at each other and swinging their big old rifles around.

Four of them got the old miner down and another one kicked him, and others was wrestling at Valerie and Meg. Francine was kicking and cussing, and one of them hit her with the side of the front end of his rifle.

I ran up and said, "You can't do that! You turn her loose!"

Then Mama come hollering, "Don't you dare take up for her!" She was pulling and hauling at me, and I admit I pushed her away.

The next thing I know it seemed like six of them had me down and one put me in handcuffs, and when I tried to fight back they hit me in the head and throwed me up in the truck.

Then Mama was kicking and scratching at the soldier boys to turn me loose. I told her, "Mama, leave off. They are only doing their job."

That done it. She looked at me like I had just stuck a knife in her stomach. "All right for you," she said. "I hope they take you straight to the penitentiary. I don't care if you never come back."

Well, the jail at Republic never would begin to hold us all from all the strawberry fields, most just boys and girls but a few older ones too, and they taken us out to the Fairgrounds where the soldiers had a camp and they put us in the livestock pens by the grandstand for the race track. It was hundreds of us just like prize hogs and cattle, and everybody around where I was at was strangers.

Then they taken us out in groups of six and run us down a line by trestle tables with some courthouse clerks and the officer of the soldiers and wrote down our names and where we come from and made us all press our thumbs in a ink pad and make a print on a paper, and they told us we was charged with breach of the peace and unlawful assembly and conspiracy and this and that, and free on bond of our own recognizance, but any that went back to striking and was arrested again was guilty of contempt of court, and we could get a year in the reformatory, and they run us out for the next bunch.

I waited for them to turn Francine loose. The sun had gone down, and it got to nine, ten, eleven o'clock at night. I waited around an old concession stand right across from the racetrack gate where all the strikers come out as they turned them loose.

She was one of the last, in a bunch with Meg and the old miner. Valerie and her pappa come up then from where they had been waiting too, and he was taking them home to Aurora in the automobile.

The door slammed, and I could see myself with a big old head and a puny little body as it started to move. I called to her, "Francine!" from not ten foot off, but I guess she never heard.

I followed in the dust a ways out the Aurora road. I was thinking now I could find work, maybe in the defense plants at St. Louis, and by the time she commenced her studies there in the fall I would have some saved up. I kept on, figuring to hitch rides.

Then Papa come along in the truck.

The Man I Threw Out the Window

Some fool boys I grew up with had already volunteered and when I got expelled from William Jewell College, that was what my family supposed I would do. But I did not study the trenches in France.

At first I was condemned to farm work. Then I came to the profound conclusion that lead for bullets was essential to the War Effort, and I might escape getting drafted if I went to work in the mines.

In the changing room I put on the muddy coveralls of a dead man, the rubber boots, and the hat with a carbide lamp in the crown. You plummet a thousand feet in a cage of wire and slats to be herded through a labyrinth of drifts sometimes in water above your knees to the rock face where you are to mine.

I watched as a man they called Lloyd held the rod and turned it after every blow, and another man swung the hammer. The diamond bit rotary steam drill was in general use by that time but in Shibboleth Number Two they still used the old system of a hand-held rod and a ten-pound hammer. The man swinging the hammer was Jared Ralls.

Lloyd Ferlyn had brought whiskey in his dinner pail and showed the effects, but he was the one who set the dynamite charge and cut the fuse.

After the blast, Luigi Bustamente and Will Skaggs and I went to work with pick and shovel breaking up the larger chunks. Then we loaded the rubble into the little hopper cars, to be hauled off by the mules who never see the light of day.

At dinner hour they questioned me.

"You know what happened to the other man?" Skaggs asked.

I supposed he meant the man whose coveralls and boots I wore.

"That rock," said Ralls, pointing to a huge slab of yellow lime-stone that lay by the hopper car track. "Smashed his head like a rotten egg . . . splattered his brains all over."

I wondered if I had offended these men in some way.

Ferlyn squatted on his haunches staring at me.

"So how come you got hired?" Ralls asked.

I said there did not seem to be anything to it. The mines were expanding because of the World War and they needed men.

"Your Pa a boss for the lead company?"

I said no.

"How come then . . . ?" Skaggs asked.

I told them a man who did work for the company went to a Caledonia meeting where my mother's people belonged and he said I might mention his name.

"Who's that?" asked Ralls.

I said Sam Curtis. He was a foreman on the other shift.

" . . . Sam's all right," Skaggs said.

They told me I was the first American hired on since the declaration of war, that the Company was hiring only foreigners because American miners were subject to the draft.

I pondered this information.

"It's to make us toe the line," Skaggs said.

"'Cause we're hard-headed," said Ralls.

Ferlyn made a sound like laughter.

Ralls said, "But Dagoes are used to it."

Luigi Bustamente acted as if he did not understand.

"Busta . . . Busta-my-butt . . . what do you think about that?" Ralls asked.

"No *capice* . . . ," Luigi said.

Both Ralls and Skaggs spoke of kith and kin who had tried to get work in the mines since April but were turned away. During the same time over three hundred immigrants were hired.

"That's not right!" I said. Surely it was against the law. Or if it was not, it should be.

The older man Skaggs spoke of renting his farm from the lead company, and they evicted him to force him to work full time in the mines. As Ferlyn continued to stare at me, I noticed half of his left ear was missing like it was cut or bitten off in some low tavern brawl. Ralls when he talked would only pretend to look at you, always glancing at Skaggs or Ferlyn or off behind your shoulder. Although no older than myself, I understood from his bitter remarks that he was already encumbered with a wife and step children.

I TOILED ON MY HANDS AND KNEES in a drift three feet high with only the guttering flame on my cap to see by. I breathed an abrasive dust of limestone and sulfate of lead that in a few years will rot a man's lungs so that he is forever coughing up blood in his phlegm and no longer fit for work. As the blisters on my hands broke, new blisters swelled up under them. My back ached. I erupted in a heat rash.

By the second day dinner hour my arms and legs had turned to lead. Only by willing it each time was I able to move one foot ahead of the other and shuffle down the drift. I felt the weight of the earth on my shoulders and myself sinking under it and was ready to quit.

As I sat watching the other men eat, Luigi poked my arm. "No *mangiar* . . . ?" he asked. It was a word like *mangy* or *mangle*.

I did not understand.

He made motions at his mouth like eating. "*Mangiar* . . . *mangiare* . . .￼" he said.

I shrugged. I had left my shiny new dinner pail under the bench in the changing room.

Luigi gave me half of his bologna and a thick slice of bread.

My eyes filled with tears.

GRANDPA SAYS DEEP SHAFT MINING is brute labor, unfit for white men. The first miners in the lead country were slaves from Haiti that the Sir d'Reno brought up the Mississippi in the time of Louis XIV, and you can still see traces of their diggings on the Mineral Fork. Then Moses Austin come in with slaves from Virginia and opened the first deep-shaft mine and built a reverberatory furnace, but he lost his money and went to Texas.

From that time until a few years before the World War most of the mining was on the old system. The rich ore was close to the surface in the sink holes and the bottoms of the narrow creek hollows, washed down in chunks and nuggets from the golden lime-stone of the highlands that you see exposed in towering bluffs. All a man had to do was dig when it suited him and from time to time sell his ore at the smelter. The big mine at the forks was a vast honeycomb of individual pits in the red earth bottoms, the pits all dug out with pick and shovel up to thirty foot deep but only ten or twelve foot wide at the top, the walls between one pit and another just wide enough for a path. For every hundred pounds of ore properly cleaned the digger received two dollars.

When Papa was a shirt-tail boy, he worked the rocker box with his two sisters washing the ore that Great Uncle James dug on his own account. They would ride in the wagon to the smelter and each get a whole dollar to spend at the store.

Now it is all deep shaft mines for the St. Joe Lead Company and if you try to sell a load of ore at the smelter, they charge you with grand theft.

At first the Company allowed you to make your score filling so many hopper cars quickly and go home early each day. In this country you can fish and hunt, cook your own whiskey, and fatten your hogs on acorns in the woods. You could live two weeks from what you made in two long days down in the mines. Men took mine work just in the winter months when farm chores slacked off.

Then the price of lead went from three cents a pound to twelve on account of the war, and the tune changed.

The Company begun to pay by the hour rather than by the day. Instead of allowing a man to go home early when he made his score, the bosses raised the score and discharged anyone who failed to make it. They discharged men for failing to appear every day of the six-day work week.

They brought in foreigners, Italians and Bohemians fresh off the boat. Blaming the draft was a sham. The idea clearly was to make us toe the line. While the local men were discharged for missing a day of work or coming in late or talking back, the immigrants reported on time, stayed the shift, did as they were told.

THE NEXT DAY dinner hour Ralls asked me, "What was you doing before you come to work in the mine?"

I said, "Farm work."

"Where at?"

I said on the home place but this was misleading. Grandpa owned three farms and had tenants to work them, and a thriving hardware store in Montgomery City. On Saturdays he preached at a country church.

"What kind of farm?"

"Corn and hogs."

"You slop the hogs?"

"I slopped the hogs, castrated them, spread manure."

Skaggs said, "I had me some stout Durocs and Poland Chinas."

"I had enough of hogs."

"Is that why you quit the farm work?" Ralls asked.

"What all do you need to know?" I asked. In fact I had worked only a short time for one of Grandpa's tenants, as a punishment after I was expelled from the Baptist College when a proctor saw me at the hotel in Excelsior Springs with a woman who was smoking a cigarette. I could well imagine what fun my inquisitor might have with this information and on no account would I volunteer it. "You are worse than my mother."

A look passed among Ralls, Skaggs, and Ferlyn.

"We are just trying to figure out how you got hired on," said Ralls.

"I told you."

"No offense," said Skaggs.

Another look passed among the three American miners. Luigi kept his eyes downcast.

"You're a liar," said Ferlyn.

"What's that?"

"You're a dirty low-down back-stabbing liar." He had a high raspy voice as if someone had choked him or struck his Adam's apple. I supposed he was trying to goad me to fight him. I groped behind me, took hold of a short-handle pickaxe.

A look passed between Ralls and Skaggs.

"We don't know that, Lloyd," said Skaggs.

"I ain't scared of no little piss-ant like him."

"You don't want them to have it over you again for fighting," said Will Skaggs.

"Lloyd killed a man," said Ralls.

I heard later that he had done time in the penitentiary.

I was not altogether sorry to hear the main-shaft whistle calling us to go back to work.

ANOTHER DAY HENRY THE FOREMAN took sick and went home early and I could tell Ralls and Ferlyn were scheming. They went off and returned and after a while they told me and Luigi to come with them.

They led us around this way and that and at least once they took us past the same hopper car with words written on it. Finally we come to the end of an old broken down drift that hadn't been worked since Methuselah and they set us to breaking up the slabs of rock on the floor that looked like a cave-in to "hand-size chunks." Ralls made a show of just how to do it, and then laughing to themselves they went and left us. Ralls called back, "We'll fetch you at quitting time."

Luigi did as he was told and set to work, but I had an idea what the game was. I told him I would be back in a minute, and set off to catch Ralls and Ferlyn while I still might.

I could hear them in the next passage laughing and then I saw the reflections of their carbide lights off the rock face. I hung back and followed along, and in no time they were back at the drift where we all were supposed to be working. They had deliberately led me and Luigi every which way around the various passages and drifts of the mine to make it seem like the labyrinth of King Minos and get us hopelessly lost.

I still had a short handle pick in my hand and am six feet tall and stout enough to take care of myself and I was somewhat hot under the collar, but I paused as it occurred to me to put on a different face.

I went strolling up to them with my pick on my shoulder and a silly grin. "Say, boys," I said, "you sure put one over on us."

Ralls and Ferlyn were surprised to see me and not sure how to act about it. I spoke to Skaggs who had remained behind and looked somewhat sheepish, "I was just bought and sold."

Will Skaggs started to speak but Ralls interrupted, "We told you to bust up them rocks."

"Poor Luigi," I said.

"The Dago . . . ," said Ferlyn.

"Well, hell!" said Ralls with a grimace.

"He can bust them rocks all night," Ferlyn said.

"Well," Ralls said, "what about this boy that don't do as he was told?"

"You had your fun," Skaggs said.

I fell in to work with them but it was not long before my relief gave way to shame. I began to wonder what Luigi was doing and how he must feel. Surely by now he knew he was the butt of a cruel prank. I could imagine him praying, attempting to find his way out and becoming genuinely lost so that no one knew where he was. The drift he was in or some other he blundered into might cave in. He could run to and fro in a panic. His light would go out.

I resolved to go find him.

But this would upset the uneasy peace I had come to with Ralls and Ferlyn. They suffered me so long as I joined them in the torment of Luigi.

I continued to break up chunks of rock with my pick.

When the whistle blew to end our shift and everyone was packing up his dinner pail and tools I asked, "What about Luigi?"

"'What about Luigi?'" Ralls mocked, and nudged Ferlyn.

"The little piss-ant Dago," Ferlyn said.

Skaggs appeared perplexed. "I suppose he's lost," he said.

"Went off and lost his self," said Ralls, "'cause he don't understanda the English."

Ferlyn laughed in his high raspy voice.

"We'll report him lost," Skaggs said.

I hung back. I was surprised at Will Skaggs.

"You so concerned for your little corn-hole buddy," Ralls said to me, "why don't you go find him your own self?"

At this I pushed past him and ran to the end of the drift.

I made a wrong turn and retraced myself, then after a moment of fear, strode up a corridor that seemed familiar and a moment after that saw a dim light.

Luigi was perched on a fallen roof timber above the rubble and water, but as I approached he drew himself up and pointed an accusing finger at me. "*Aver Vergogna!*" he said.

I took this to mean I should be ashamed of myself, and I was. I tried to explain that it was like a snipe hunt and you had to leave one fellow holding the bag, but he did not need me to explain anything for him.

"*E un' gioco grosso.* Ho-ho-ho."

I hung my head.

"*Ragazzi crudeli . . . tu anche!*"

I believe he was saying we were crude boys. In my heart I knew that was charitable. Ralls did not care if a ton of lead fell on him, and Ferlyn would laugh his scrannel laugh at the news.

"*Tu anche . . . que sol' meliore sape.*"

I nodded. I should know better and was heartily ashamed. Yet I did not see how I might have conducted myself differently except to have remained with him, and that I was not prepared to do.

ON TUESDAY JULY FIRST, a train arrived from St. Louis with over four hundred Italians and Bohemians.

At the end of the shift the bosses paid us off and we were discharged.

A clerk started to call me out of the line but another clerk said, "No. Him too."

We stood in small groups talking and milling around in the dirt street outside the company offices for Shibboleth Number Two, where the changing room was on the second floor. Then Will Skaggs, Lloyd Ferlyn, Jared Ralls, and his cousin Eddie headed down Water Street to a blind pig, and I went with them.

Other men from our shift were already there drinking steadily. The same thing was on everyone's mind and we talked of little else. Flushed with a shot of whiskey and a beer chaser, I delivered an opinion. "They set us one against the other," I said, "just to lower our pay and stuff their own pockets!"

Ralls exchanged a look with Will Skaggs as if to say we have a philosopher in our midst, but I learned this kind of talk at my father's knee when he was organizing for the Cigar Makers in Kansas City and worked for the *Labor Tribune*.

Eddie Ralls said, "It's against the law!"

I said, "You'd think it would be."

We heard rumors of it. We had seen it coming. But when the

Company actually did it, firing able-bodied Americans on the excuse we could be drafted and hired immigrant foreigners to replace us, we were truly amazed. The enormity of it took time to sink in.

A man came into the bar room and shouted, "The Italians bragged on it! They're saying, 'When the Americans go to the war, we get the jobs . . . and we getta their women.'!"

It was like lighting a match to straw soaked with coal oil. A roar of outrage went up from the men and we poured out into the street. Miners erupted from other taverns and pool halls up and down the hill from Breton Creek and we formed a crowd at Bingham's corner that grew rapidly as the report spread. "Well what are we going to do about it?" one man shouted.

"Send them back where they come from!" said another, and that became the cry. "Send the Dagoes home!"

The crowd surged across the creek to the Company offices for Shibboleth Number Two at the end of Prospect Street and rushed into the changing room and started throwing Italians out of the windows.

I was caught up in the spirit of it and pushed and shoved and hollered with the rest—though I had in the back of my mind how I was acting a part to be sure that I did not become an object of their wrath. Any one of the terrified men we easily drove before us might have been Luigi, who shared his dinner pail with me. I did not see him or read his name afterwards in the *Post-Dispatch* on the list of foreigners who were hurt. I like to think he gauged our temper and stayed at home that night.

I went up to St. Louis then and pretty thoroughly dissipated myself for several weeks until sure enough I got drafted, and they shipped me off to the Argonne Forest.

Peter Leach

Peter Leach, currently living in St. Louis, Missouri, is winner of the 1989 *Nebraska Review* Fiction Award. His short fiction has appeared in *Virginia Quarterly Review, Minnesota Review, Indiana Review, Kansas Quarterly, Arkansas Review, Artful Dodge, River Styx, Best Little Magazine Fiction,* and *NYU Press.* An NEA Creative Writing fellow, his work has also appeared in *Prize Stories: The O. Henry Awards.*